L.J.
HAYWARD

Dealing in Death
Copyright © L.J. Hayward

Cover Art: L.C. Chase, lcchase.com
Editor: May Peterson, maypetersonbooks.com/editorial
Layout: L.C. Chase, lcchase.com

ISBN: 978-0-6487846-0-9

First Edition
September 2019

Also available in ebook. ISBN: 978-0-6484460-3-3

L.J. HAYWARD

Dedicated to Riina and Yuuko,
For your undying enthusiasm for Jack and Ethan and your
support and friendship.
Happy birthday!

TABLE OF CONTENTS

I attached the scope with a soft *click*, then ran my hand over the Assassin X, swiftly checking the assembly. Everything was smooth and ready, so I set it to my shoulder and looked through the night-vision scope. The target came into view. A balcony on the third and top floor of an apartment building. There was a single chair on it, and tonight, for the first night in the week I'd been watching it, it was occupied.

He was home. At last.

Jack Reardon sat with his feet up on the balustrade. They were bare, his toes curling and flexing in the warm, early autumn night air. He wore only a pair of track suit pants, his hair still wet from a shower, hanging in thick black curls over his forehead and neck.

Seeing him again was both a balm and a pain. Knowing he was hale eased a tension I'd been carrying since leaving him in the desert. I didn't understand the effect Jack had on me, having never before experienced that flood of warmth and joy that just looking at him created in my body. Nor the surging physical need for him to be close to me. Jack had awakened something in me that hadn't quietened since we'd parted ways. Just the thought of him was enough to rekindle those sensations. And that was why it was also a pain. I would never have the chance to feel those things firsthand again. This was as close as I would ever get to him now.

So I drank him down as much as I could. His brown skin, long legs, narrow hips and broad shoulders. If only he would lean forward so I could see the tattoo of the St. Thomas Cross on his left shoulder blade. Instead, he slouched in the chair, mouth slack, staring at something distant. The Sydney skyline, the faint spread of stars, a horizon he'd never reach?

I'd seen that despondent expression before, when Jack had thought I wasn't paying attention. At the torture shack, as he'd named it, and after the fight, when he'd realised I—his enemy and a cold-hearted assassin—was his best hope of surviving. It had reappeared during the night and day that followed, but not since then. Not even when I'd betrayed him at the compound, or while he'd been tied to that chair as my primary target, Samuel Valadian, taunted him. When we had parted ways at the old homestead, he'd been determinedly stoic. Two months later and I was seeing that despair again.

My hand itched to leave the trigger guard and reach out to him, to smooth away the lines around the corners of his mouth, to trace the shape of his eyes in the hopes they would light up again for me. In humour or anger or lust. Anything so they wouldn't look empty anymore.

He had been a target. A means to an end. He was supposed to be dead by my hand. I was not supposed to miss him so much my body hurt.

But I wasn't here to ease that ache, as much as I wanted to. I had come to do what I should have done in the desert—protect him.

Dropping the angle of the rifle, I scanned across the front of Jack's apartment building. There was faint light shining through one window on the second floor, and apart from it and the brightly lit common areas of the building, it was all dark. The leaves of the trees and hedges along the front of the building rustled gently every now and then but otherwise, it was all still. The building wouldn't be difficult to breach, nor would Jack's apartment, I was certain.

I scoped the street and, sure enough, found my true target. A sniper rifle and perch on a neighbouring building might be the easiest way to kill Jack, but that option wasn't available to Two. All Sugar Babies shared white irises, fixed pupils and a heightened night vision, but the condition also exaggerated other issues, such as Two's short-sightedness. He'd never been any sort of marksman and had instead perfected hand to hand combat. Jack was a very good fighter, but he was no match for Two. I couldn't let him get anywhere near Jack.

Placing the crosshairs in the middle of Two's face, I snapped a photo of him through the scope with my neural implant—basically a smart phone grafted to my temporal lobe—then sent it to Two.

He blinked when my message came through, then a slow, cool smile curled up the corners of his mouth. His connection *ping*ed into my head a moment later.

"I'm impressed, little brother. How long have you been waiting?"

"Long enough I began to doubt your insistence that you are the best amongst us."

Two laughed. *"As your inability to finish your jobs lately caused me to doubt your second best status."* He motioned in Jack's direction. *"This one is supposed to be dead. I overheard your debrief with Zero and thought I would finish the job before you get into too much more trouble with the bosses."*

My heart gave a single, hard thump at the thought of Jack having to face Two. I would do anything I could to make sure that never happened.

"Let's go somewhere else to talk," I sent.

In the crosshairs, Two looked up at the balcony above him. His face was blank, but I knew him well enough to guess at the thoughts running through his mind. Calculations on how to deal with me and Jack. I could do the math just as well as he could. He would have to deal with me first.

"Fine." Two turned away from Jack's building and walked towards a steel-blue Audi RS5 parked further down the block.

I kept him in sight as I dismantled my Assassin X and then slid down the rope I'd hung over the side of the building. Hitting the ground, I went to the car and found him in the passenger seat.

"I know better than to take the wheel when you're in the car." Two smiled as I settled into the driver's seat. He dangled the keys from a finger. "You also know this city better than I do, since you come here at least once a year to race."

Careful to not react to the statement, I took the keys and started the car. It rumbled into life and dropped into a satisfying purr. Not quite as sublime as Victoria, my Aston Martin Vanquish S Coupe, but decent all the same.

I tried not to make a show of my racing habits. It was impossible to think that the Cabal and therefore Zero, our handler, and my siblings weren't aware of it, yet it was purely my thing, nothing to do with any of them. It was an escape from the world the Cabal had tried to drown me in. That they hadn't entirely succeeded was a small victory I needed in order to survive. Letting Two know how much it meant to me would destroy the peace it gave me, because there was no doubt in my mind that he would use it against me.

Not wishing to alert Jack to anything unusual, I pulled out sedately and cruised down the street. Two was quiet as I wound us through Leichhardt in the early hours of the morning.

Why had Jack been up at this time? Restless sleep or still trying to reverse our mostly nocturnal patterns while in the desert? Or had he brought someone home with him? Someone who kept him up until two a.m. with activities that required showering after?

I shook those thoughts away. Jack had no reason not see anyone else. What we had shared had felt special to me, but that didn't mean it had been to him. He'd called it mutual attraction and that had certainly been true, but unlike me, Jack probably felt that for any number of people.

"He was supposed to die," Two said as I turned onto the highway and headed west. "That was the job."

"No, the job was to determine if he knew anything about the person protecting the primary target. He didn't."

"And when you proved that, he was supposed to die. All targets have to be eliminated, One-three. You know that as well as I do." Fingers drumming on the passenger door window, Two frowned at the passing scenery. "Zero should have ordered you to return and finish the job. I shouldn't have to do it for you."

My fingers tightened around the steering wheel at the thought of Zero giving that command. "Zero doesn't define our job parameters."

"He does enforce them, though."

"But he didn't send you here to kill Ja—him."

"No, he didn't. I still have to do it though, because you didn't. Or was it because you *couldn't*?"

I kept my gaze directly ahead. The highway was mostly empty but to let my attention drift away would only confirm Two's suspicions.

"You let this target distract you. Why, One-three?" When I didn't answer, he continued. "You're better than that. I *made* you better than that. You always finish the job. Why didn't you finish this one?"

He sounded genuinely curious. I had no doubt he truly was, just as I knew I would never be able to explain it to him. I didn't understand it myself. Even if I did, Two never would. He simply had no capacity to understand.

"The target may be useful in the future. Zero agrees," I said.

The look Two gave me was cold and knowing. "Only because you killed the primary target too soon."

"He threw himself on my knife."

Which I could have pulled away but hadn't. In the moment the target had lunged towards me, I'd flashed on him bending me over the desk and unbuckling his belt while muttering about making sure I knew who owned me. The screen in front of me had shown footage of Jack in that white room, tied to a chair, tossing his head in anger and confusion. It'd made me believe he felt something more than simple attraction for me. It had let me understand that I didn't need to let Valadian think he could own me anymore. So instead of keeping him alive and prying information out of him, I'd let Valadian run himself onto my knife.

It had been a failure, but a satisfying one.

And Jack had come incredibly close to paying for it. I had to make sure Two wouldn't come after Jack again.

"I made a mistake," I whispered.

"Yes, you did." There was a hint of resigned weariness in his tone that sent a shiver down my spine. I was familiar with that sound, and what it meant.

The rest of the drive was silent. It was nearly mid-morning when we reached the exfil location. I'd sent the request for pick up hours earlier and the chopper would be here soon, touching down in this hidden valley west of Sydney. We would get onboard and it would take us to a private airfield with a jet, or to a ship offshore, and we'd slip out through the gaps so no one would even know we'd been here.

I got out of the car, reconciled to what was going to happen.

"I didn't think I'd have to do this again," Two said as he came around to stand in front of me. "I'd thought you would have learned by now."

"It was a mistake."

His hand cracked across my cheek. I went with the blow, lessening the impact. A second and third slap, delivered fast and hard, didn't give me that option. Two lowered his arm and stepped back. I didn't move, head knocked to the right, blood trickling into my mouth from my teeth cutting into my inner cheek.

I could have fought back. I burned to fight back. To catch his wrist, twist his arm and kick his feet out from under him. I couldn't, however. Quite apart from him being the superior hand to hand combatant was the fact that if I did manage to best him now he would only retarget Jack as a means to punish me. Two was frustrated and confused and he blamed me for these upsetting emotions. This was how he dealt with them.

By the time the chopper landed, my left eye had swollen closed, I'd had to wrap my shirt around the knife wound in my arm and Two had to help me limp to the aircraft. All the while, he told me he was sorry for hurting me and that he wouldn't have to if I would just stop making mistakes.

All that mattered was that it was me Two said these things to, and not Jack.

EIGHT MONTHS LATER

The car pulled up outside the front of the shed next to my cottage in the Wachau valley in Austria. I wiped my greasy hands on the already dirty rag tucked into the waistband of my jeans and stepped back from Honey's engine. She was a Lamborghini Huracán I'd rescued from a human trafficker in Hungary. Apart from a few performance issues I'd sorted out, the most work I'd done had been on her paint job. The piece of filth who'd owned her had had half naked warrior women painted on her bonnet and flames along her sides. Now she was pristine white. A new beginning.

Leaning against her side, I waited while the driver got out of the van, opened the side door and pulled out a ramp. A moment later, Zero wheeled himself out and down, his powerful arms easily propelling his chair across the gravel drive and into the dim interior of the shed. His greying blond hair was buzzed almost down to the scalp and a scar cut from his left temple, under his sunglasses and across his nose to the right side of his mouth.

"One-three," he said in greeting.

I nodded in acknowledgement.

It hadn't been that long since I'd last seen him. After Two and I had been picked up west of Sydney, I'd been confined to a Cabal black site while I healed. Two and Four had been sent out to trace Samuel Valadian's partners in the hopes one of them would know who had been protecting him. As of a month ago, when Zero had told me I could finally leave, they hadn't had any luck.

"Your brothers still haven't managed to complete their task," Zero said in German.

"I didn't think they would."

"The bosses want the job finished, no more waiting."

I concentrated on getting a smudge of grease off my hand, not wanting Zero to see any hint of the hope that flared at the thought of getting to complete the job. "I have a plan." I'd had little else to do while recovering from Two's punishment.

The corner of Zero's mouth turned up slightly. "I thought you would." He reached up and took off his sunglasses to clean them. White eyes locked on to me. "What do you need?"

"I quit."

Nine carefully set her SIG Sauer P226 down on the workbench and turned to face me. "You what?"

I smiled at her horrified tone and loosened the bolt on the front wheel strut of her white Ducati SuperSport S.

Her reaction was much as I'd expected. As had been Seven's, our sister. Three months ago, as we'd cleaned up the mess left at her Vietnam home by myself, Jack and a Burmese drug lord, I'd told her my plans to leave the Cabal—properly this time—and start a "real" life with Jack. Seven had swallowed the news with her usual calm, told me to be careful, and then blown up her house to eliminate the evidence of what had happened there. Six weeks after that, when my request to meet face-to-face with Zero had been granted, I'd been pleasantly surprised by his response.

"I'll inform the bosses."

That had been it. No objection, no reasoning, and supposedly I was free of the Cabal. Of course, that was pretty much what had happened last time as well, and to my shame, I'd gone back to them within months. That wouldn't happen this time. I was older and stronger. I had used that time to gather everything I needed to be independent of them. This time, I had Jack. A thought that flooded me with warmth, even if it also left me a trifle shaky.

"Repeat that for me." Nine pretended to clean out her ears. "Not sure I heard you right."

"I quit. I'm no longer an assassin, for the Cabal, or anyone else. You do realise that if you didn't treat your bike so roughly you wouldn't need me to fix it constantly, don't you?"

A bullet casing flew across the room and hit the side of my head. "I've seen you drive. I've been *in* the car when you drive. Don't tell me how to ride."

"The difference is, I can maintain my cars." I picked up the casing and pocketed it. Mostly to keep the space tidy, partly so she couldn't use it as, well, ammunition against me again.

"And you maintain my bike," she pointed out primly. "When you're in town, which you haven't been lately. A lot. Is it because of *him*?"

Focusing on the bike let me move through the guilt her words inspired. I hadn't been to Johannesburg as much lately, and yes, it was because of Jack. Normally, I would split my down time between the Wachau valley in Austria and here in Johannesburg. I had been in South East Asia a lot recently. Which *was* closer to Jack in Sydney.

"I have been spending time in Sydney, yes."

Nine was the one sibling I felt most comfortable talking about Jack with. Not because she was sympathetic or encouraging, but because after she snarked at me for neglecting my brotherly duties—fixing her sadly abused motorcycle mostly—and teased me about cuddling and more *intimate* activities, she left the subject alone. Seven argued that I was being stupid and reckless, but then helped in her own way. Whenever I crossed paths with Four, I didn't talk to him about Jack at all. Two and Ten I avoided any way I could, personally and professionally.

"Sorry," I added. "I know I haven't been here as much lately. Is Au—"

"*That's* not what I meant." Nine put her gun back together with a rapid staccato of clicks and locks that echoed the deadly potential in her tone. "I meant, is he the reason you quit?"

"Of course not."

Nine's spark of anger turned into a full-blown smirk. "I think it is. I think you want to go be his househusband and cook for him and wait by the door wearing nothing but an apron—Hey!" She tumbled off the stool at the workbench to avoid the wrench I'd thrown at her. Landing in a crouch, she had her SIG pointed at me.

Shrugging, I turned back to her bike. "You threw something at me."

It was nearly thirty seconds before the safety on the gun clicked on. "A bullet casing, not a deadly weapon." She stood and put her gun back into the holster hanging low on her right hip. "I still think I'm right. You're *quitting* because of the spy."

"I left the Cabal well before I met Jack."

"Right. Left the Cabal." She almost choked on her laughter.

With a final grunt, I got the last bolt off and the front tyre dropped free. I rolled it a little way away and laid it down. Then I stood and went to wash my hands in the bathroom.

The layout of my safe place in Johannesburg was much like that of the one in Sydney—much like all of them, truthfully—with a workbench along one wall, space for my car and workout areas next to it. Living area with kitchen, bed, and bathroom were to the other side. By the time I emerged from the enclosed bathroom, Nine had stopped laughing and stood over the dislocated wheel, hands on hips, looking between it and the rest of the Ducati.

She was barely big enough to ride the bike, small and delicate beside the Ducati, but looks were very deceiving in Nine's case. There was startling strength in her slender body, and a spine made of the toughest material known to mankind. Of all of us, she was the only one who'd ever bested Two hand to hand on a regular basis. Much of that ability came from her small stature, and being able to dodge Two's big limbs, but the rest of it was pure skill and canny intelligence.

With her Cape Coloured heritage, Nine's territory was Africa and she'd never failed the Cabal—apart from five months several years ago when she fell off everybody's radars. However, even with that little hiccup, Eve Garrote sat at number five on the John Smith List, and while Seven also worked under the moniker, that high ranking was largely due to Nine. Seven's most valuable talents to the Cabal were her hacking and technical skills. Of all my siblings, Nine was the one I trusted the most—if she got the order to kill me, she'd let me know about it before she attacked.

Nine's fine black brows furrowed together. "Are you going to finish this?"

"Eventually."

White eyes narrowed, she followed me into the kitchen. "What does that mean?"

"It means I'm hungry. Do you want dinner?"

Her little nose wrinkled up. "Did you cook it?"

"Yes. Never fear, I'm getting better."

Opening the oven where I'd been keeping the food warm released a cloud of spicy, meaty aroma. My stomach rumbled appreciatively, echoed by Nine's quiet moan.

"Potjiekos?" she asked warily, and when I nodded, said grudgingly, "It actually smells good."

For which I was eternally grateful. If Nine was going to agree to my request, I had to make sure she was as amenable as possible. She was small but she ate like someone twice her size, and while she had no interest in cooking herself, she was highly critical of it in others.

Nine crowded me at the counter as I dished out the potjiekos. "Did you stir it while cooking?"

"No."

"How long did it cook for?"

"Four hours on a low heat."

"Bread or rice?"

I nodded to the brown paper wrapped parcel and ceramic serving dish on the dining table. "Fresh bread and butter."

Eyeing me suspiciously, Nine sat, unwrapped the bread and started slicing it thickly. "You want something."

"Am I not allowed to simply do something nice for—"

"You *want* something." Nine accepted the big bowl of food from me. "Don't bother asking until I've eaten. If this is as good as it smells, I might just be willing to listen."

Settling into the seat opposite my sister, I hoped it lived up to her expectations. After some of the discussions I'd had with Zero while cutting all ties to the Cabal, there was a high possibility I would need someone's help in the coming years. Seven would have helped, I was certain, but after watching the destruction of her Vietnam house three months ago, I didn't want to annoy her so soon.

Nine dipped the buttered bread into the thick mixture and took a hesitant bite. Expression unchanging, she chewed, swallowed, and repeated. Unable to tell anything from her face, I tried the potjiekos. The dish was one of Nine's favourites and I'd come to enjoy it as well. There had been attempts in the past to cook it myself that had never passed muster with Nine. This one tasted much better than the previous ones. The flavour of each ingredient managed to remain separate from the others, while also blending into a rich, spicy whole when chewed.

Though tentative at first, Nine took larger and faster mouthfuls. Half way through, she began to nod as she chewed. By the time she'd finished, scrapping up the last of the juice with a slice of bread, she was smiling.

My stomach relaxed around the small amount of meat and vegetables I'd managed to eat. The signs were leaning toward Nine's agreement to help me out.

"That was . . . acceptable," she announced magnanimously when her bowl was nearly clean enough to skip washing.

Acceptable was good.

"You may ask me whatever it is you want, and I shall listen to it." She held up a warning finger. "I will hold back on my response, however, until you produce dessert."

Shaking my head, I pushed aside my half empty bowl and made a pot of tea. The familiar actions and blooming aroma settled my nerves.

This had been my childhood within the group of Sugar Babies the Cabal had gathered for their malicious means. I would give and give in the hopes that one of my siblings would give back even a small portion of what I offered. In my naivety I'd not understood why the other children hadn't responded how I'd hoped. It hadn't been until years later, when I better understood what had been done to us, how it had affected us, that I accepted I would never receive normal affection from the others. They simply could not fathom the concept, not even Nine, the most well-adjusted of them all. Yet the pattern had been set back then. I gave, they took and, occasionally, returned a morsel.

I wanted more than a crumb of attention this time, but I hoped Nine would help me all the same.

"Jack has asked me to live with him." I set the pot and cups on the table.

Nine blinked, then blinked again. "What?" Before I could answer, she leaned back and laughed. "I was right! You want to be his husband

and pretend to be normal. That's crazy! He doesn't even know your real name and he's asking you to live with him."

Waiting out her hilarity, I poured the tea and wondered if she wasn't right.

It *was* crazy. The sort of life Jack was envisioning for us wasn't possible for someone like me. I was too different. Too dangerous. Too damaged. Jack didn't know my real name. He knew I'd been born Paul St. Clair, but that name hadn't truly been me for over twenty years.

"What does he call you, One-three?" Nine asked between cackles. "Honeybunch? Sweetiepie?" Her eyes went wide and she asked in a faux-horrified whisper, "Sugar baby?"

I shuddered. "No. He calls me Ethan. Or Blade when he's cranky." Or overly aroused.

A fine brow arched incredibly high. "Oh, wow. I bet that makes you feel good."

"I've come to . . . appreciate the Ethan, at least." I couldn't look at her reaction to that, so I got up and fetched the dessert from the fridge. "Peppermint crisp tart?"

Normally, Nine would have taken the foil container from me with all the grace of a rabid wolf, but instead I got only silence as I presented her favourite dessert. Nine just stared at me, her face inexpressive.

"You said yes, didn't you," she said, tone flat and quiet. "That's the favour you want. You're going to go live with this spy of yours and you need me to make sure Two doesn't kill you for it. Like he tried when you came back from the desert."

Two hadn't been trying to kill me then. That had been punishment for finding someone else I wanted in my life. Someone I wanted more than him. I cut into the tart for something else to focus on, rather than the thought of how Two would react if he knew what I was planning on doing.

"That's correct, and I plan to do so honestly. Thus why I finally cut all ties with the Cabal. I won't be taking any independent jobs either. However, I don't care for my own safety, but Jack's. Without access to the Cabal's resources, I won't be able to keep track of any threats towards him as well as I used to. That's what I want to ask you to do."

Nine stared at me, then let her gaze drop to the big portion of tart I'd levered out of the container and offered up. With a sigh, she pushed her empty bowl across the table and I slid the slice into it.

After a couple of bites, she finally spoke. "What exactly do you expect of me?"

I hid a sigh of relief in a sip of my drink. "Just to keep an eye out for any hints Jack may be targeted for any reason, and if a ticket is put on him, to pick it up before anyone else, so I have a chance to void it before he's in any real danger."

Nine shrugged and scooped up another piece of tart. "A Meta-State spy is a bit below Eve Garrote's standards. She's at number five, you know. She might *lose* points just for picking up a ticket on someone like him."

Meeting her gaze, I said steadily, "I'd do it for you. I *have* done it for you."

"That was different."

"Not by much."

She growled at me and finished off her desert in a couple of huge mouthfuls, then gestured over her shoulder. "Who's going to fix my ride if you're off being *normal* with him?"

Confident she was onboard now, I gave her the name of the local mechanic through whom I sourced most of the parts I needed for Raquel, my BMW Roadster. "And it's not like I'll never be back. I don't only come here for jobs," I added lightly.

Snatching my unfinished dessert, Nine poked her tongue out at me. "You weirdo."

Nine's help secured, I went and finished correcting the suspension on her Ducati. She lounged around, complaining about how much she'd eaten, then raided the fridge for more tart. When the bike was ready and she was preparing to leave, I caught her before she could get on and gave her a brief hug.

"What are you doing?"

Her body was stiff and I had a momentary flash to how Jack must feel when I couldn't relax in his arms. It hurt, but as he did with me, I held on. I usually gave in, but Nine didn't. I let her go and stepped back.

"Saying thank you," I whispered.

"Weirdo," she muttered again, but I wasn't offended.

Until Jack, I hadn't been comfortable with signs of affection either. I'd yearned for it, yes, but hadn't experienced it from another human in so long it had been a foreign concept.

Nine shook her head and slung a slender leg over the seat of her bike. "I'll keep an eye out for information or tickets on your spy, but only if you'll admit something to me."

I handed over her helmet. "Which is?"

"That he's the reason you quit."

It appeared we were back to this again. "I quit previously, well before I met Jack."

"Hah! That was just you negotiating better pay and working conditions." She winked at me and patted the fuel tank of the Ducati. "Thanks for that, by the way. But!" She held up a finger. "If this is you *really* quitting then there is only one reason why. *Him.*"

"Jack is not why I'm doing this."

Nine rolled her eyes and pushed her helmet down over her head. Via the implant, she sent, *"By the way, because I couldn't quite believe you were back in J-burg, I checked up on the spy and he's currently in Bangkok."* Her tone grudgingly shifted into one of mild approval. *"Looks like he might actually catch the Messiah. Maybe that's why the Cabal gave you their blessing to leave. As a reward for Loverboy for doing something they couldn't."*

I barely got the door opened before she was roaring out of the warehouse.

CHAPTER TWO

Nine's intelligence proved true and Jack was still in Bangkok when I left Johannesburg a couple of days later. I spent some time in my safe place in Kuala Lumpur, then when I couldn't hold back any more, I went to Sydney.

Hoping Jack's job didn't take him too much longer, I holed up in a hotel with security I mostly trusted and waited. I read and watched a few of the movies Jack couldn't believe I hadn't seen. I would have preferred to watch them with him. Perhaps it was the teasing I missed, or the pleasure of watching Jack watch me, his hope that I enjoyed this thing he liked barely concealed. By day three, however, the charm of having nothing pressing to do wore off and I couldn't distract myself from the thoughts swirling through my head any longer.

The fact I was bored so soon into my new life of leisure didn't bode well. Likewise, the idea that I was merely passing time until Jack returned from overseas worried me. Was Nine right? Was I changing my entire life just for Jack?

There was fear, too, on the flip side of that coin. What if Jack wasn't enough? What if, a month or two down the track, I discovered nothing would help me and I couldn't *not* be an assassin?

Desiring a distraction I began a search of the local wreckers, seeking a hidden gem that would catch my eye. Not one of my personal cars had been bought off a show room floor. All of them had come from wreckers or were rescues from bad homes. All of them had needed work to make them as-new, or as close as humanly possible.

It was how I'd found Victoria, poorly used and abused, her engine burned out and body ravaged. I'd had to tow her to my Ingleburn safe place, where it took me nearly a year to restore her to pristine condition. Of all my cars, she was my greatest achievement. I would have called her Phoenix if I could have.

Sadly, there were no treasures quite as sublime as Victoria but I did find a late model yellow Holden Monaro in need of some loving care. It wouldn't require as much work as Victoria but I was rather keen for a distraction by then and the pickings were incredibly slim.

It took the better part of the following day to find a suitable garage I could rent in order to work on the Monaro. By the time I had her successfully housed in a small industrial complex that rented out individual garage spaces, I hadn't thought about Jack and our future together for roughly fifteen minutes. Taking the engine completely apart helped, as did making a shopping list, and I was back touring wreckers when a notification came from Nine early on the morning of day six.

Messiah successfully captured and en route to Sydney Office. Loverboy surely accompanying him.

Sure enough, within a couple of hours of staking out the Neville Crawley Building in Darling Harbour, I saw an armoured truck followed by two dark-coloured, unmarked 4WDs enter the underground carpark. Without being able to see into the cars, I still knew Jack was there.

He was home and I felt both elated and worried. I wanted to see him so badly, to hear his voice and let his touch relax me as nothing else could. I still needed patience, however. Jack would need to process his prisoner, which would require him jumping through endless hoops and dealing with the red tape barriers bureaucracy invariably created.

Thus I took my time getting ready and then, finally, fetched Victoria from storage.

Somehow, she'd become closely entwinned with Jack, and not only because I'd let him drive her when we went to the Gold Coast. Or left her in his care when I'd had to scramble out of the country so suddenly. It was a mildly unsettling connection between sinking into her red leather seat and knowing I would soon be with Jack. I mean, I enjoyed driving a great deal, but I'd never felt aroused by getting into a car before. Not even the Maclaren I'd let loose in on the autobahn.

The mild arousal plaguing me on the drive over didn't exactly disappear when I got to Jack's apartment, but it did take a back seat to the swell of warmth and contentment at simply being here again. The last time, I'd believed I wouldn't be back, but it felt right that I was. I had missed this place, with the brown leather couch a touch too soft to be perfectly comfortable and the dining table Jack had pinned me against more times than we'd shared a meal on it. The kitchen where I'd watched him prepare butter chicken, before inhaling the curry and promising Jack my entire body in return.

I drifted through the rest of the apartment, ostensibly checking the security, but really indulging in a flood of good memories that eventually and inevitably led me to the bedroom. My clothes were off and I was on the bed before my thoughts had caught up to my actions. The plan, such as it was, had been to wait for Jack in the living room, fully clothed, in case he'd changed his mind. I did, however, manage to stop myself from burrowing into the sheets, seeking a hint of Jack's scent. It would have been a fruitless search. He'd been away for three weeks and the sheets felt unslept in. Had he changed them before he left just in case I arrived while he was gone? The possibility that he had didn't help that low-level arousal.

Aiming for distraction, I found a novel I'd left in the bedside table drawer. It was one I'd read a couple of times but it helped keep some of my attention from focusing on the apartment's security system. The moment Jack entered his code to unlock the door, I would know. Until then, I only had to be wary of uninvited parties.

Of which there were none before a soft *ping* sighed through my head at nearly ten p.m.

Jack.

Heart racing, fingers twitching, I waited as he closed and locked the door, then walked calmly into the kitchen. Oh dear. He was angry with me. Why wouldn't he rush to find me otherwise? I suppose he could have missed Victoria in the garage but I doubted it.

What felt like an extraordinarily long wait later—but was in truth perhaps a minute—Jack appeared in the doorway. He had a bottle of water in his hands, a travel-rumpled cast to his suit and hair, and a very neutral expression. His gaze skated over me, pausing on my underwear for a moment—probably noting that I wasn't unpleased to be viewed—and down to my socks, which he focused on while he unscrewed the lid of his water.

After taking a small drink, Jack said, "Ethan."

I met his gaze directly and in that moment, I knew he still wanted me. Those beautiful brown eyes had never been able to hide anything from me. I had wondered at first how Jack managed at his job without giving everything away with a single look, but careful observation had revealed that not everyone could read him as I did. I tried not to consider that it was because the first time I'd looked into his eyes he'd been on the edge of breaking down—thanks to me. It hurt to think that Jack's honesty with me was solely because I had left him no other option in the desert. I wanted to believe it was his choice to show me so much of himself now. If it wasn't, then I was as bad as the people who'd tortured thirteen children into becoming merciless killers.

I didn't want to be that person to Jack. To anyone.

Thankfully, the growing bulge in his trousers assured me he was happy to see me. Oh. *Very* happy to see me. I smiled.

"Jack."

"It's been a while."

The way he winced as he spoke reminded me he had every right to *not* be happy to see me. "For which I'm sorry. I certainly hadn't meant to take so long to get here. Thank you, though, for respecting my request."

"Yeah, about that." Jack dropped his gaze to the bottle. "I was going to call you tonight."

I locked my body down, otherwise I would have thrown myself at him and all the things I wanted to say would never get said. "You were?"

"I needed . . . to know you were okay."

The rest of my body I could control, but a bigger smile broke through. "Well, it's lucky I needed . . . to know you were all right, as well."

Jack smiled back, eyes scrunching up as he struggled not to. "Can I ask why it took you so long to . . . enquire about my wellbeing?"

We had to have this discussion but that didn't stop me from wanting him closer. Much closer. Close enough so I could touch and whisper and hold and promise.

"You may. The clean-up took longer than I anticipated. Afterwards, there were a few personal matters I had to take care of."

"Such as?"

Well, I had invited the questions. I couldn't back out now, so I surrendered to the moment, relaxing my arms and fully accepting my decision.

Jack took a step forward, suddenly on alert. "Ethan?"

"I quit, Jack."

"You what?"

This was it. I had to give this part of myself to Jack if he had any chance of accepting me so completely in his life. He had to know exactly—or at least more thoroughly—what he was getting into.

"I haven't taken an official job in over eight months, Jack. There's been no . . ." With an effort, I tried, "I haven't *needed* to work since we started seeing each other. The—for want of a more accurate word—compulsion just hasn't been there. You once asked me if I liked what I do. *Did.* The better question would have been *why* I did it."

And suddenly, there were very few blocks left and all the words tumbled out. Words I'd never spoken to anyone ever. Not to Nine or Seven or my brothers. They all knew, viscerally, the driving need to follow our training. To be successful, but also, to survive. To protect the Cabal's "investments." They all knew, too, about the desire to be free of the Cabal. My desire, if not theirs. But Jack didn't know those things, so I told him, and I told him how I'd "quit" once before. And failed.

"But something in me wasn't right. I couldn't *not* do anything, Jack, and the only thing I knew how to do was stalk and kill. Only when I was on a job did I feel balanced. Like I was real. So I went back to it and two years ago, I found something else that made me feel balanced. Someone who made me feel real."

"Ethan," Jack whispered.

"Please, Jack. Let me finish." If he didn't, I doubted I would be able to do this again.

All the thoughts Nine had sparked about doing this only for Jack, not because I wanted it for myself, needed to be let out and Jack was the only one I trusted to hear them. They were half formed and probably made little sense, but Jack seemed to follow along well enough because when I said firmly, "Jack, I'm here and I don't want to leave," he launched himself at me.

For an instant I flashed into defence mode, but quickly understood Jack was simply trying to get close, to touch me and reassure himself I really was here. When he lay completely on top of me, our bodies aligned, and his face was pressed into the side of his neck, he let out a long sigh and melted.

Well, most of him did. There was one very hard part of him pushing insistently into my thigh. A part of him I wanted pressing very insistently into a different part of me. *This* we knew how to do, and do very well. Naturally, we ended up naked and Jack effortlessly drove me wild with his touches and words and lips.

Afterwards, we lay in a filthy tangle of arms and legs, Jack's cock still inside me even as he tried to take his full weight off my back. I kept him as close as possible, fingers digging into his flesh if he dared attempt to move. He learned to stay put quickly.

"So fucking happy you're here at last," he mumbled into my shoulder.

"Hmm, yes, I'm rather pleased with the situation as well."

Jack snorted. "Yeah, I figured." He gave a little thrust with his hips, sending a jolt of slightly awkward pleasure through me.

"Fine," I conceded. "You may move if you wish."

Mimicking my *hmm*, he whispered, "I don't wish."

I smiled into the pillow. "Good. You get a fifteen minute rest. Make the most of it."

This time, Jack laughed hard enough he slipped out. He took the chance to roll me over and settle back down on my chest, the mass of his sweaty, black curls resting just under my nose. I breathed in deep, filling myself with the much-missed scent of him. I did, however, find hints of other smells that weren't entirely usual.

"Have you changed your deodorant?"

"No, why?"

"You smell ... fruitier."

"Is that a euph ... oh shit." Jack scrambled up and sat back on his heels. "Look, it was for work, okay? And I haven't had time to shower since, but I swear, he didn't get really close to me. Well, he may have sat on my lap. Or danced on it, just a bit, but it did nothing for me. I swear. Thought of you the entire time. And then I sedated him."

I eyed his desperate pleading sceptically and raised an eyebrow. "You let him give you a lap dance, *then* sedated him?"

"It wasn't like that! The lap dance was in the main room. I waited until we were in his private room before—" Jack caught sight of the grin I was trying so hard to hide. "Fuck you, Blade." He rolled backwards off the bed and stalked out of the bedroom.

I couldn't help it. I laughed so hard I curled up, arms wrapped around my middle.

"No, seriously," Jack called back at me. "Fuck you."

Between gasping chuckles, I got up and followed him. He was in the bathroom, dampening a washcloth and muttering under his breath about not being appreciated for the sacrifices he made for the Meta-State. His shoulders were tense as he rubbed down his arms, which mollified my laughter, even as it gave me a spectacular view of his tattoo. Calmer, I laid my palm over the St. Thomas Cross, fingers spread to reach to the very ends of the stylised symbol.

"I'm sorry, Jack. I couldn't help myself." When he didn't brush off my hand, I leaned against him, reaching around to take the washcloth away from him. "You don't need to do that. It's a very faint smell, and more alcoholic than perfumery, regardless."

Jack stiffened, the line of his spine going straight against my chest.

"Jack?" What had I said this time?

"It's okay." After a moment he relaxed, sagging against the sink. "It's just been a long three weeks with no breaks. And I'm starting a new job in the morning that I'm not looking forward to. Sorry." His hand covered mine on his chest. "Having you here helps a lot, though."

Pressing a kiss to his shoulder, I pulled back and turned him to face me. "Then I'm doubly glad I'm here for you. Come on, back to bed."

"Don't you want me to shower off the smell of a Bangkok rentboy first?"

There was a bitter twist to the words that worried me but, not wanting to hurt him again, I shook my head. "It doesn't bother me. And you'd only need to shower again in the morning."

Dragging his feet, Jack nevertheless caught on and smirked at me. "Yeah?"

"Yes. Your fifteen minutes are nearly up."

CHAPTER THREE

We shared the shower in the morning, then ate together. Jack, rushing out the door with his helmet under his arm, slapped a quick kiss on my cheek, gave me a shy smile like he couldn't believe his luck, then was gone.

And I was back to waiting and worrying.

Jack had mentioned over breakfast that his new job was an undercover one. He'd been avoiding them since the desert. Since I'd used him for my own ends. Did he resent me for that time? Even subconsciously? I did feel bad for what I'd done, but couldn't truly regret it because it had been exactly what I'd needed to do to get an almost impossible job done. Of course, I wouldn't do that sort of thing again to Jack, knowing him as I did now. Feeling what I did for him. I wouldn't be manipulating anyone else, either, given my current situation as a non-assassin. Which once more left me with the question . . . what was I now?

The only thing I could convince myself of, while wandering through the empty apartment, was that I was an owner of a poor Aston Martin Vanquish S Coupe that hadn't been driven much in four months. I dressed in the suit I'd worn the day before, wrote a note informing Jack I'd be back later, and left. First stop was the storage unit where I kept Victoria, and several changes of clothes. In jeans and a T-shirt, I then went to where I had the Monaro and gave Victoria a thorough going over. Then I washed and polished her until she was gleaming. All of which didn't quite keep me as distracted as I wanted. My thoughts kept flitting over the worry that with me constantly underfoot, Jack wouldn't be able to ignore the terrible things I'd done to him when we met. That, sooner or later, he would realise us living together was a mistake, and if that came to pass, and if I didn't find something outside of Jack's circle of influence, I was on a slow slide into madness.

When Victoria was showroom ready, I washed and changed into a suit and contacted Dejana. If this life with Jack didn't work out, I would need all my resources ready to go.

Fortunately, Dejana had a cancellation in her schedule and could fit me in later in the afternoon. Her office was in the Capita Centre in the CBD, a striking construction squeezed into a narrow space in an already crowded street, making up for the lack of footprint with an impressive height. Dejana's office—or at least the place she met with the likes of myself—was on the 22nd floor. The space was furnished only with a desk and two chairs. There were no filing cabinets, no sideboard, no ficus in the corner and no paintings on the bare white walls. Apart from the basic furniture, the only things in the room came in with the visitors. There was a large window behind the desk, showing an impressive view of the roof of the building across the street. Where, I was certain, at least one sniper waited with their crosshairs on my head the entire time I sat opposite the impeccably turned out woman before me.

"It's been a while, Saint." There was a trace of accent to Dejana's words, perhaps Eastern European, yet she'd been situated in Sydney for as long as I'd been coming here. It was the only hint to her heritage, however, as she'd cultivated a pale complexion and paired it with artificially silver-grey hair twisted into a neat knot at the base of her skull. I was fairly certain her green eyes were contacts, as well.

"And I'm afraid it will be a long while again, once we've finalised a few things." I kept my hands on the armrests of the chair, in plain sight of her and her insurance on the roof over the way.

Dejana nodded as if losing my business had been expected. I didn't know how she got her information, but she had connections that rivalled some of the higher members of the Cabal. In fact, I couldn't be sure she *wasn't* part of the Cabal, but over the years she had treated me as honestly as any of us could in this game. I—and all of her other clients—paid very well for her services, and her silence.

"Your accounts. Do you wish to close them all?"

"Yes and have everything transferred to several new ones." I made to reach into my jacket's inner pocket, watching her carefully. Only once she'd given me a stately wave of one hand did I retrieve a business card. "These are the details."

Her white lacquered nails clicked as she pinched the card by one corner, glancing at the printing before handing it back. "It'll take a few months to move some of the larger amounts. Do you have a time frame for completion?"

"No. Just as quickly as you can without drawing undue attention."

Dejana nodded once. "There will be my usual fee, plus ten percent." She gave me a moment to protest the added amount, and when I didn't she nodded again. "I'll let you know when it's all complete. Was that everything?"

"Yes." Business concluded, I stood and prepared to leave, automatically scanning the top of the building across the street.

What appeared to be a pair of limp, gloved hands were dragged back over the edge of the roof.

With a curt nod to Dejana, who showed no signs of anything amiss, I left quickly but not hastily. I took the stairs two and three at a time, though, and once outside, hurried across the street, but slowed to a brisk walk through the tiled foyer of the other office block. Pressing the down buttons on all of the lifts to delay my quarry, I headed up the stairs, again at a run and startling the few people I passed. I remained wary as I went, wondering if the person who had possibly taken out Dejana's sniper was on their way down, even as I went up. I passed no one suspicious, which didn't surprise me. Whoever could take out someone Dejana would have hired wouldn't have been so amateur as to rely on the building's stairs or lifts to escape.

I wouldn't have.

Sure enough, when I broke through the door to the roof and scouted the space, I only found a dead body and a HK417 rifle. However, on the next building over—a decent jump but manageable— the door to the stairwell had been propped open. A simple case of the killer forgetting to remove the wedge under the door? Or a deliberate act to draw me after them?

Trap or not, I didn't take the bait. Whoever it had been didn't appear to want to harm me. Otherwise, why kill Dejana's sniper and not take a shot at me?

"Unfortunate."

I turned to face Dejana. She stood over the body, her white pantsuit pristine despite having hustled after me fast enough to arrive mere minutes later.

"Do you have any idea who may have done this?"

Dejana merely cocked a finely shaped brow, shades darker than her hair, at me.

Conceding to her point, I checked over the body. There was a black-tufted dart in the back of the man's thigh, whatever it had been loaded with fully injected. The dart itself was rather generic and would prove of little worth in tracking down the killer. Likewise, the man's broken neck was nothing unique, though the fact it had been accomplished in a single, swift move meant the killer was strong and most likely trained. Again, telling Dejana this was a waste of time, so I merely stood and brushed off my hands, preparing to leave. She would have the means to clean this up without alerting the authorities.

"It appears I have a job opening." Dejana's tone had dropped from her usual calm evenness into a wry twist.

I stopped, watching her from my periphery. Her stance hadn't changed, but she was looking at me directly now. A pale brow quirked up enquiringly.

Snorting, I continued toward the stairwell. "I've quit."

"You've said that before."

Keeping the instinctual reaction to eliminate the threat to a minimum, I turned and faced her, expression locked down. I'd left the Desert Eagles in Jack's gun safe at the apartment but carried three knives and years of hand to hand combat experience.

Dejana didn't flinch. She wouldn't have lasted as long as she had in this business without learning to face danger without hesitation. The merest hint of vulnerability was like a drop of blood in shark-filled waters.

"I need protection." Her voice was back to the one she'd used in her office. All business. "Insurance to do what I do." She indicated the dead body at her high heels. "Clearly."

I agreed with a single nod. "Good luck with filling the position."

"I know why you want your money moved as you do. I've been expecting your visit for some time now. It would be a shame if I failed to do this for you because I was dead."

"I'm sure you can find someone else just as capable. I've quit. Completely."

Dejana gently nudged the body with the back of one foot. "And yet you rushed over here the moment you noted something wrong. Hardly the actions of someone who doesn't have an interest in the game anymore."

"In the game, no. In my own safety, yes. This doesn't appear to be move against me."

"Fine. Best of luck finding someone else to move your money for you. If it is even still in your accounts when you find them."

"I don't need the money that badly."

She shrugged. "Perhaps not, but I believe you do need help escaping those who think they own you."

I locked down the sudden worry. "I've already done that."

"Are you certain? When two hands shake, both must let go."

Behind the sunglasses lenses, my eyes narrowed. *This* was the sort of manipulation and machination I'd hoped to leave behind forever. It didn't, however, stop her from being correct. I'd done everything I could to leave the Cabal, but that didn't mean they'd let me go.

"Can you do this?" I asked quietly.

The hint of a smile was smug. "I don't promise what I can't deliver, Saint."

Dejana's reputation was solid. It was the main reason I came to her.

Without another word I returned to the body and picked up the H&K rifle.

"You were my last appointment for today," Dejana said coolly. "I won't need you until tomorrow." From a pocket, she produced a card and a pen. Writing briefly, she said, "Meet me at this address at ten a.m. I'll have a phone for you that only I have the number for. Bring the rifle."

I took the card, memorised the address and handed it back, as she had done in the office earlier.

"I'll have the first of your transfers completed by the day after tomorrow, one of the smaller ones, to give you some walking around money," she said as she turned to leave.

"Knock off the extra ten percent from your fee."

Dejana glanced back at me, that eyebrow raised again. "Three percent."

"Seven."

She laughed and kept walking. "Five. See you tomorrow, Saint."

CHAPTER FOUR

As I got back to Victoria and stowed the rifle under the passenger seat, I marvelled at how short my peaceful life as a retired assassin had been.

Jack would kill me if he found out.

I spent the rest of the afternoon at a gun range on the outskirts of the city, testing the rifle. It performed superbly, having been very well cared for. Afterwards, I left the weapon in my storage shed, returned to the hotel room, which I had until the end of the week, and showered to remove all traces of my evening activities. Then I sat on the bed to tie my shoes and just did not get up.

I'd given in far too easily to Dejana's demand. Zero hadn't exactly said the Cabal had agreed to my terms, but he hadn't said they objected, either. I was free already.

Unless I wasn't.

I couldn't risk it for Jack's sake. For my sake. I'd wanted this for a very long time, before I'd met Jack even, and this was the best possible way for it to happen. My only recourse was to continue with this ill venture and hope it didn't cause trouble with Jack.

By the time I'd worked through the dilemma, it was quite late. Grateful I hadn't given Jack a definite time, I returned to Leichhardt and found him already in bed. I suppose some of the worry showed because he watched me warily as I undressed.

"You can use the wardrobe," Jack said. "And we can reorganise the tallboy to fit your undies in."

"You wouldn't mind if I did?"

"Of course not. I thought this was what we were doing. What we talked about. You being here for more than a flying visit. Staying here."

Right then I realised this was the first time either of us had mentioned it since reuniting last night. Some of the tension in my chest eased just hearing it aloud. "I suppose I wasn't sure if that was still what you wanted."

"Jesus, Ethan. Just toss your clothes in the laundry basket and get your stupid arse in bed."

Which I did. We play wrestled for a while, seemingly leading toward sex, then Jack's mood turned pensive, so we talked about our days, which included Jack moaning about his assignment. I sympathised but couldn't help but wonder what other couples chatted about at night. Surely not the trials of going undercover. Jack sounded so morose about it that I aimed to distract him in as pleasant a way as I could, trailing my fingers in suggestive patterns over his chest.

"Christ," he moaned mid-sentence and pulled me on top. "Quit teasing and just get on with whatever you want to do."

"As you wish, Jack."

Jack faux-grumbled as I retraced the trail marked by my fingers with lips and tongue. His erection from earlier came back remarkably fast, giving me something to rub against. His crankiness faded almost as fast as his cock rose, his hands sliding up and down my back, strong fingers digging into my arse and grinding me on him harder when I dared to pull back.

I made sure every inch of his broad, muscular torso knew just how much I'd missed it. Jack ran his hands up my back, the heat of his touch curling my spine. He held me there, poised above him, and kissed my exposed throat, slowly making his way downwards. As he went, he pushed me back, following until he was sitting up and I was in his lap. I arched against the circle of his arms and Jack groaned before sucking one of my nipples into his hot mouth. Gasping, I pushed into the sensation, one hand on his head, the other bracing myself on his thigh.

"God," Jack mumbled against my skin, "I love this. You on my lap. Moaning like that."

"Hmm. I would never have guessed." Which got my arse spanked.

"Behave," he growled over my startled gasp.

Cheek stinging with a pleasant warmth, I asked, "Or?"

"Or this stops now." He tried to look stern, but it was ruined when his lips twitched a second before he gave me another swat.

Surprisingly enjoying the sensation, I wriggled my hips exaggeratedly. "But I thought you liked lap dances."

"You little shit."

Jack surged up, intending to tip us over so I was on the bottom. Laughing, I twisted, trying to get free before he pinned me. Somewhere in the manoeuvre my foot got caught under Jack's arm. He tipped too far in the wrong direction and over we went.

When everything stopped moving, we were on the floor beside the bed, me on my back, Jack half on top of me.

After a moment to take stock of the situation, I muttered, "Perhaps we need a bigger bed."

Jack snorted and propped himself up on one elbow so he could leer outrageously. "I don't know. We have *all* this floor space." He gestured grandly, then rubbed his still hard cock against my thigh. "We're not going to fall any further. Let's make the most of it."

"But, Jack." The words turned into a moan as he shifted completely on top and resumed his plan of attack on my nipples. My legs automatically parted and wrapped around his hips. Cocks slipping and sliding together, I thought perhaps he had a valid point.

Then Jack thrust his hips just right, my back arched, scraping my shoulder blades against the hard surface, and the back of my skull connected a bit too sharply with the floorboards.

"Shit." Jack sat back on his heels and hauled me up, pulling my head to his chest. "You okay?" He ran his fingers through my hair, gently seeking any damage.

The mild pain faded with the tender touch. I leaned into his chest, wallowing in the sensation.

"Ethan? Does it hurt anywhere?"

"Hmm? Oh. No, I'm fine."

After a moment, Jack chuckled and pushed my face off his chest. "Okay, stop drooling on me. Let's take this back to the bed. Third time's the charm?"

We stood but before getting into bed, Jack checked my back and arse, rather thoroughly, for injuries.

"Still perfect." His hands lingered on my hips and he moved up behind me, hard cock aligning flawlessly with my crack.

About to correct his "perfect" comment, I got distracted, both by him grinding against me and the recliner in the corner. An image formed in my head and I drew Jack to the chair.

"What are you . . ." His question trailed off as I turned him and pushed him into the recliner. "Ethan?"

Without a word, I arranged him to my preferences, arse on the edge of the seat, legs spread but not too wide, arms up and hands holding on to the headrest. Throughout, Jack watched me with curious lust, his cock hard and leaning on his taut abdomen, tip glistening with pre-come.

"Ethan?" he tried again when I stepped back to admire my work.

"Jack," I returned, restraining the urge to give up my silly idea and just fall on him.

It never failed to amaze me that Jack's body could affect me so viscerally. From that first moment in the shed in the Great Sandy Desert, seeing his long, lean frame still attempt a slouch while tied to a chair had captured my eye. And when the subterfuge was over—for him at least—and he'd let the military man show, all straight lines and hard angles, I was no less caught and had been ever since. I still dreamed about the devil costume he'd worn for one of his jobs.

"Is this going to be a don't touch, don't talk type fuck?" Jack's arms flexed as he tested his grip on the recliner, as if settling in for a long time.

"No." I started moving, just a little sway, and touched my hips and thighs with fingertips, skimming my skin in swirls and loops.

Jack swallowed and his gaze locked onto my hands like a targeting system. "Then what is it?"

Unable to stop the smirk, I said, "Something I think you'll enjoy," before turning and backing onto his lap, still rolling my hips to a silent rhythm.

After a stunned moment, Jack whispered, "Oh fuck." The soft old leather squeaked under the pressure of his hold and his groin jerked up a small fraction. Then, breathless with lust and perhaps a touch of amusement, he said, "You're giving me a lap dance?"

I rubbed my arse along the line of his cock. "Since the last one was cut short, I thought you might—ow!"

The ringing of the light but smarting smack to my rear was drowned out by my laughter.

Jack's murmured, "Crazy bastard," was warm with affection, though, and the slide of his hand up my spine, slow and deliberate until his fingers teased the nape of my neck, was pure heat and desire.

"Half right, Jack." I tipped my head back, inviting his touch to go further and his fingers curled through my hair, tugging but not painful. I let him pull until my spine was sharply curved, my arse still rocking on his lap.

"Jesus," he hissed. "So fucking beautiful."

Jack's other hand landed on my hip, not commanding, just connecting, feeling the motion through splayed fingers that traced over the top of my flexing thigh, rolling hip bone and under the curve of my arse cheek. I groaned, sounding wanton and desperate. I *was* wanton and desperate.

Every touch was like the spark of a livewire. I was shaking as I continued to move on him. A cynical part of me, all but smothered by raging lust, said I must look ridiculous, sliding around naked on another man's lap. Yet I didn't care because Jack was touching me like he would never stop and making sounds that shivered in my skin and set my nerves to humming. For him, I would do anything.

"Turn around."

I was sure he meant it to be an order, but it came out pleading and broken. There was no hesitation in me, however. I turned and Jack pulled me back onto his lap, straddling him on my knees. He pulled me in until our cocks were pressed together between us. One hand spread across my upper back, his thumb teasing my hairline. The other went low, curving around my arse, the tips of his fingers sliding over and over my sensitive entrance. I didn't think I was dancing anymore, but I was certainly moving. Forwards to rut against his cock, backwards into his fingers, and Jack was keeping a beat with his words, "Fuck. Yeah. God. Perfect. Christ. Ethan. There," uttered between kisses and nips and licks to my neck, chest, arms.

I felt whole and real and alive.

I felt safe. Secure enough to let it all go and just exist.

"Ethan?"

The concern in the word brought me back to the moment. Everything was still in motion. Jack slowly and irrevocably taking me apart with his touch and putting me back together with his voice, but now he was looking at me, head tilted back slightly, lips parted as he panted, dark brows pinched together in worry.

"You sort of went away, in here." Jack tapped my forehead gently.

"Quite the opposite," I murmured.

Jack's smile was downright devilish. "Yeah?"

"Yes."

"Good."

"Very good." I traced a finger over his eyebrows, then down around the outer curve of his eye socket, across his cheek and along the side of his nose. The stubble around his mouth made my fingertip tingle, the softness of his lips soothing it away gently. Jack met my fingertip with the point of his tongue, making me gasp, then again, louder, when he caught my finger and sucked.

His gaze held mine, staring unrelentingly into me as his lips and tongue did wonderfully awful things to my finger. Each stroke of his tongue sent an equivalent shiver down my cock. When he hollowed his cheeks and sucked hard, my hips jerked in sympathy. He licked and nibbled and sucked faster and I panted along with his rhythm, my free hand inching ever closer to my aching cock.

Jack caught my hand and put it behind my back, holding it there. He frowned sternly, then went back to his torture. I whimpered plaintively but it failed to move him to mercy. It was barely a minute longer before I was wriggling on his lap, seeking more friction against his belly, more pressure from his cock next to mine. Another minute endured, then I broke.

"Jack. Jack, please. Suck my cock. Please."

All suction ceased and slowly, Jack slid his mouth off my finger. "Say that again."

I knew what he wanted to hear but played dumb, though the heat rushing up my neck and cheeks surely gave me away. "Say what?" The words were barely audible.

"What you want me to do." A hint of a smirk curved his lips upwards.

My hair was sure to burst into flames at any moment. "You heard me."

"Yeah. I'd like to hear it again though." Jack nuzzled into my chest. "Because unlike last time you spoke dirty to me, I think you mean it this time. I don't care about that, though. Just need to hear you say those words again, right now." Big, beautiful dark eyes cast a soulful look my way. "Please."

For a man who could be rather unforgiving, Jack absolved me of so many sins I could sometimes forget I wasn't good enough for him.

"Jack," I said slowly and clearly, "suck my cock."

Any sense of accomplishment I may have felt vanished in a flurry of Jack repositioning me until I was kneeling on the armrests of the chair, my groin right at his face level, aching cock pointed rather obscenely at where it wanted to be.

"Yeah." Jack licked his lips and stretched his jaw. "Yeah, perfect."

Then he closed his mouth over the end of my cock.

Hands braced on the back of the chair, I closed my eyes and let Jack work his magic. All the sensations he'd fed into my finger were amplified ten-fold and I was embarrassingly close to coming very swiftly. Jack seemingly knew this, however, and slowed until I wasn't panting and trembling so much I was in danger of falling from my perch. Then he slid his mouth all the way down until his nose was in my pubic hair and the head of my cock was pushed into the back of his throat.

"Jack," I whispered.

Then he swallowed. Again. And again.

I floundered, half out of my mind with the jolts of pleasure racing through me, half with panic that Jack would choke. He didn't, thankfully, and pulled his mouth off slowly, licking up my shaft the entire way.

"Jack." It came out shaky and broken.

He must have heard the concern in my voice because he nuzzled into my groin, kissing and humming against my fevered skin. "It's all good. Love doing that."

It sounded sincere and I knew—absolutely *knew*—Jack wouldn't do anything he didn't want to, and yet I couldn't help but wonder why he wanted to. Or if he really didn't mind that I couldn't return the favour.

Head tilted back, chin resting on my hip, Jack smiled up at me. His lips were wet and eyes bright with excitement. "Can I keep going? Want you to come in my mouth."

I shouldn't agree. This was too much when it was all one sided . . . and yet, selfishly, I nodded.

Jack grinned stupidly, laid a trail of kisses and nips across both hips, then sucked my balls into his mouth and wiped any and all thoughts from my head. Damp fingers slid between my arse cheeks, stroking over my entrance in time with the delicious pulling on my cock as he went back to sucking it. His name tumbled from my mouth on gasps with silly frequency, but even biting my lips didn't stop the need to praise him, so I touched him. His head, shoulders, cheeks, flexing biceps, any part of him I could reach, to let him know it was him, just him, only him, who could ever do this to me.

"Yeah," Jack mumbled whenever he could, as if hearing my silent declaration. "Yeah. Fuck. Yeah."

Then he did it again, all the way to the base of my cock, and swallowed. I came in a terrifying rush of heat and pure light, shouting his name as I spilled everything I was into him.

When I regained some cognition, I was settled back on Jack's lap, my head lying listless and empty on his shoulder, his arms wrapped around me, hands gentling up and down my back. I stirred and Jack kissed my temple.

"Welcome back. I was worried you'd passed out, the way you were drooling."

I managed a weak slap on his arm, which only made him laugh outright.

"Brute," I muttered.

Jack shifted, prodding his steel hard cock into my inner thigh. "You could pay me back."

Not so long ago I would have worried he meant for me to return the fellatio, but I knew better. Knew him and trusted that he would never force anything sexual from me. Heat flared in my belly at the thought of wrapping my hand around him and watching as I brought him to orgasm.

Strength and purpose returning to my body, I shifted until I was straddling him again. I held up my hand, palm towards him and with a dirty expression, Jack licked it until it was slick with his saliva and whatever of myself lingered on his tongue. Wrapping it around his straining cock, I gave him a slow, firm stroke and he moaned.

Doing it again, I leaned in and whispered in his ear, "Turn about is fair play, after all."

Jack groaned and bucked. He didn't last long, and I didn't want him to, needing to see him fall apart for me. It was amazing and beautiful, and afterwards he crushed me to his chest and held on like he would never let go.

Or so I hoped.

CHAPTER FIVE

When I woke up, Jack was gone and the apartment was quiet. The spark of worry for my security came and went so swiftly I almost missed it. No matter what I said to assure Jack, his place still didn't meet the usual standards I held my safety to, but that fact was slowly losing importance the more I was here. Perhaps in a month or so of continual residence, it would vanish altogether. Which set off a secondary worry that I might lose other parts of myself in the process of adjusting to this new life. Practically, I understood that such a thing wouldn't be entirely bad, and yet I'd lived—and survived—as I had for so long, change was potentially dangerous. If not deadly. Yet Jack wouldn't leave me alone if he thought there was any threat.

Right now, the only threat was being late for Dejana's meeting.

Dejana had been in this business for a long time and had never made waves. Well, not with anyone powerful enough to threaten her outright. Which could mean she had protection from someone who had the clout to keep her safe, but she still needed the immediate security of someone watching her back. The simple fact that her sniper had been killed meant she needed it. And if I wanted to have a real life away from the Cabal, it was now my job to keep her safe.

As I contemplated wearing the same suit I had yesterday, I had to admit Jack was right. I needed to actually *move in*, or this was going to be rather time consuming. In the end, I borrowed a pair of Jack's jeans and one of his flannels, a red checked one I loved seeing on him. It was clean, but I imagined I could smell him on it all the same. It felt intimate to wear his clothes, to know he wouldn't mind that I did, and to think of the look on his face if he saw me in them.

Breathing through the desire those thoughts inspired, I left the apartment. After the attention I'd given her the day before, Victoria ran beautifully on the way to my storage unit. However, we picked up a police tail along the way and I spent a while losing it before getting to my destination. It was not unusual these days. Victoria's anonymity had been destroyed in a race with several police cars a year before, but the job had worked out perfectly. Well, as close as it could when Jack decided to get involved.

My head was clear when I reached the storage unit, where I changed into one of my specially designed suits that allowed me to wear the Desert Eagle harness with both guns. It also had compartments for the back-up Glock 17, my knives and a garrotte. Even as I put the suit on, I tried to imagine it hanging beside Jack's everyday clothes and a weird little thrill went through me. It was a lovely thought but as with every change I was making lately, it came with a dose of apprehension. I was certain Jack wouldn't care to know the suit had been made to make my job of killing targets easier, but would it be a constant reminder to him that I was, technically, the enemy?

Either way, I needed it today and it felt traitorously good to slip into it once again. After days of wondering what my life was becoming, this was something I knew as well as breathing. Chances of actually having to kill were slim, but the mechanics of the situation were ones I could do with my eyes closed—literally if required. H&K rifle disassembled and packed into a briefcase, I left Victoria behind and caught a taxi to the meeting spot.

Once at the Royal Botanic Gardens I walked to the Australian Rockery Lawn. There were a few joggers on the paths, a couple of families with prams and little children. Two different groups of school children were being herded around by teachers and garden staff. No apparent threats, but sources of potential victims, so I catalogued them all carefully as I went.

I was an hour early for the meeting, which was about an hour later than I usually liked to be, but normally, I wouldn't have been comatose from two exceedingly good orgasms the night before. However, it had left me refreshed so my reconnaissance went fast and smooth.

The Australian Rockery Lawn was within walking distance of the Opera House, and therefore had a spectacular view of the iconic white sails and the wide harbour. The grass was vibrant green and the native plants on the rock walls were muted shades of gold, silver and red. I'd mentally mapped the area and planned the fastest escape routes by the time Dejana appeared.

Today's suit was ice blue, making her hair seem more white than grey. She carried nothing but a proud bearing, and unless there was a derringer in her cleavage, she came unarmed as well. Trusting me to ensure her safety. Just as I was trusting her to deal with me fairly. At least as fairly as anyone did in our realm of the world.

"Saint," Dejana said as if there had never been a doubt about my presence today.

I nodded back and fell into step beside her.

"This meeting shouldn't be any trouble," she murmured as we walked towards the Opera House. "Hold back so you don't hear anything, but be seen."

Another nod. As we rounded a curve, I picked the target immediately. He stood further along the path with a woman and two children. The youngsters, a toddler and school-aged boy, played on the grass, laughing delightedly, while the adults stood with their heads bowed towards each other, their conversation not a happy one to all appearances. Dejana slowed and I fell further behind as she carefully approached them.

Noting Dejana, the man hastily straightened and turned toward her, ignoring the hand his wife put on his arm. I recognised him as Grant Owen, one of the youngest members of the opposition's front bench. Talk was that he'd only risen as far as he had because his political party wanted to draw in the new generation of voters with a handsome face they could better identify with. And that was the only dubious thing I'd heard about him. So why was he dealing with someone of Dejana's reputation and skills?

Reminding myself this was not my true concern, I stayed back while Dejana and Owen spoke. Likewise, the woman split her attention between the children and her husband, the worried frown never leaving her face. It deepened remarkably when she glanced at me, then she moved closer to where the children still tumbled about excitedly.

The exchange didn't last long and I saw no threats the entire time, though when Dejana gave Owen a final, precise nod, his hand twitched toward a pocket. Dejana merely quirked an eyebrow at him and he relaxed his hand again. Without a word, she turned her back on Owen and started walking back the way we'd come. I let her pass me, waited several beats to make sure Owen knew not to follow, then turned after Dejana.

We made it back around the curve of the land without trouble and were back in front of the stone walls when Dejana stopped. She retrieved a small phone from a pocket and gave it to me.

"Thank you for today. I'll have the first of your smaller transfers finalised by the weekend. I'll give you a call when I need you again."

"You don't require protection back to your office?"

"No. You were here more for appearance than any other reason today." She kept walking. "Keep the phone on you, Saint. You'll never know when I might need you."

I gave her a decent head start and then followed her through the gardens, keeping out of her sight and awareness. Yes, I was curious why she felt safe enough without me now, but also I took my reluctantly accepted job seriously and didn't want anything befalling her before she could keep her promise. Along the way, we passed a TV crew heading towards the Rockery Lawn to, I learned via the chatter of the interviewer into her phone, meet with Owen and his family.

Tamping down any curiosity I concentrated on the immediate task, making sure Dejana got to her waiting car safely and that she wasn't followed. Back at my storage unit, I changed into Jack's clothes, tucking the Glock into the back of the jeans under the flannel and keeping the wrist sheaths with their knives, not quite ready to go without a weapon. Then I started packing some clothes to take to Jack's apartment.

Somewhere in the process, I realised I was stopping every few items to check the wrist sheaths, making sure the knives slid free with a flex of the joint and wouldn't get caught on the sleeves. If I tugged on the cuffs of Jack's flannel any more they were in danger of pulling free. I settled for rolling up the sleeves and continued.

When I found myself reaching for the Eagles' webbing, I forcibly stopped myself. One gun and two knives were overkill when I was inside a locked storage unit and under no immediate threat. Yet the thought of packing anything more made my stomach tighten. So I left it and went to the rented shed and worked on the Monaro, which proved a better distraction.

As I was finishing up, someone walked by the front of the closed roller-door. By the step-step-grunt combination, I knew it was the complex manager, Ken. Or someone who'd mimicked his gout-ridden walk. Whoever it was stopped just past my shed, turned, and came back, slower, paused by the smaller door, then moved on. As Jack would have said, not suspicious *at all*.

Swiftly going *sideways*, I pulled up the footage from the tiny camera I'd mounted over the door. Sure enough, the person outside was Ken Warren, his balding head shining with a coating of sweat as he hesitated at the door, one hand raised to knock, the other running over his smooth pate and down to grip the back of his neck. After another moment, he muttered, "Screw it," and knocked.

Coming out of the light trance, I rolled out from under the Monaro as he knocked again and called out, "Mr. Scott. Are you in there?"

"Just a moment." I slipped on my glasses and opened the door to him. "Sorry, I had my head all the way inside the engine and didn't hear you." I used an Australian accent and leaned casually against the doorframe. "Did you want something?"

"Uh, yeah." Ken unsubtly peered past me into the dark interior of the shed. I didn't need much light to see by without my sunglasses on. "Just wanted to see if you were doin' okay. Got a Monaro, huh?"

Ken had seen me drive it in barely a week ago. "Yeah. Fixin' it up for a mate. It's in pretty good nick already."

He nodded enthusiastically for a few seconds, then said, "And everything with the shed okay? No worries with anything? At all?"

"It's all good, thanks. Anything else you needed?" He was fishing. For what, I didn't know yet. I'd hired this space from him because he'd been referred to me by a contact who repurposed stolen car parts in this very complex, and Ken had indeed appeared supremely uninterested in the tenants. All of which made this whole conversation very suspect.

"No, no, just checking in." The sweat on his head had increased and it rolled down the side of his face. He swatted it away irritably. "Okay, look. It's just that a cop was here today, asking questions."

"About me?"

Ken shook his head. "Nah. Well, maybe. He described you pretty well but didn't have a name or anything."

Was this connected to the police car that followed me this morning? "Did the cop say why he was looking for someone who looked like me?"

"Nah. Just that they were interested in finding you . . . ah hem, whoever."

Interesting. "Well, thanks for letting me know. I'll keep an eye out for anyone who meets the description."

Ken nodded a few more times, taking the chance to look into the shed again, before I purposely stood back and started closing the door. With a parting, "Ah, okay, sure," he backed up and step-step-grunted his way back towards his office.

CHAPTER SIX

I checked my weapons. It wasn't at all comforting that the local police had an interest in me. They knew Victoria, yes, but they shouldn't have any reason to come after me. I hadn't acted professionally in Sydney since Jack and I had exposed the traitor within the Office. If Director Tan was serious about keeping on my good side—which was dependent upon my good behaviour within his borders—he shouldn't allow the police to threaten me without an incredibly good reason.

Unless this was about Dejana. Yet no matter which path I followed, I could not find a logical reason she would have for selling me out. If it was connected to her, then it was probably tied into the death of her sniper. It was possible the authorities had images of me in the office building where he was killed, but for them to know of the killing, Dejana's clean-up crew had failed spectacularly, which seemed highly unlikely given the longevity of her career.

I was doubly cautious making my way back to my storage unit, where I quickly packed a few more clothes before returning to Leichhardt. It was dark by the time I got there but Jack wasn't home. I checked the security system and the footage from the front-door camera; no one but Rocco Cesare from next door had approached the apartment all day, and he only to knock a couple of times before heading out on his morning walk with his dachshund, Short Round. Unsure of what the police interest meant, I didn't unpack anything and instead hid my bag under the bed in the spare bedroom. If anything went sideways, I would be able to clear out of Jack's life easily that way.

Unable to settle even in this familiar, cherished space, I did something I hadn't done in years. After making a clear area in the living room, I went through a tai chi workout. It was something I'd taught myself after the Cabal had set us loose on the world to make our own way between jobs. They had succeeded in creating a group of—mostly— loyal assassins skilled enough to do any job, but they hadn't given us any means of dealing with the world they cast us into. Perhaps the others didn't need a way to decompress; they had, after all, seemed much more capable than I. Yet within months of being on my own, I'd felt close to flying apart at the seams. I had thought once I was on my own, I would have been able to free myself from the Cabal. I had been wrong, and tai chi was one of the ways I'd learned to deal with the consequences of my choices.

I was calm when Jack got home, yet his presence centred me further, even as the appreciative rake of his gaze over my body awoke me in other ways. He joined me readily enough, his own tension bleeding out of his body with each move, though he still appeared a touch worried when we were done. Hoping it was nothing to do with the police attention on me, I distracted him with dinner negotiations. While waiting for it to be delivered—which didn't sit well with my security needs—I found my eye being drawn to the picture of Jack's parents he kept on his bookshelves.

It was such a beautiful image of two people in love, an undoubtedly happy memory for Jack of the mother he'd lost years before, and the father he was slowly losing to dementia now. A telling image of the man Jack was today. It needed a better position on the shelves, not tucked away in the corner. Which threw off the symmetry of the shelves, requiring further rearrangement. When I caught Jack watching me with a bemused expression, I paused, worried he would object. His smile only grew wider, so I continued.

Jack's preoccupied mood faded through dinner, to the point he laughed at my reaction to the mess he willingly made of his meal, but returned sharply later. We were watching "Black Books," which I had seen before but, since Jack enjoyed exposing me to the things he loved so much, I pretended I hadn't. I found I was enjoying it much more with Jack beside me. Until he went silent and the colour faded from his face.

"Jack? Are you all right?"

"Yeah, sure. Of course. Why?"

He was lying. "You went very quiet and pale."

"I don't go pale," he scoffed.

"You do, Jack. Are you getting sick?" I set down the beer bottle I'd been flipping idly and touched his forehead, checking for fever. Sick Jack could be amusing, but he could be hurtful as well and for my sake as much as his own, I didn't relish going through that again.

He took the empty beer bottles to the kitchen. "I'm fine, okay?"

Each repudiation only convinced me further something was happening inside his handsome head. Determined to find out what it was, I went into the kitchen, but before I could make another attempt, I was lifted up and set on the countertop.

"Jack! What the devil are you doing?"

He was between my thighs and pressed against my chest without me even considering refusing his advance. His wet tongue set my skin to shivering from shoulder to ear. "Think that's pretty obvious."

Teeth joined the assault on my earlobe, the nibbles sending sparks of electricity down my spine, but when he started sucking on the flesh behind it, I melted even as my cock hardened. Jack knew exactly how to take me apart, effortlessly and oh so thoroughly. I struggled to recall what we'd been talking about. Oh yes, what he was attempting to distract us both from.

"Indeed. However, I should probably have asked, why?" His broad back was warm under my hands, muscles sliding silkily as he moved against me.

"I thought I was the one who was supposed to fish for compliments. How does 'you're so fucking hot I can't resist' sound?"

Which would have otherwise convinced me if his body had been more responsive.

I pulled back and held him in place with my hands on his cheeks. Those glorious brown eyes couldn't hide him from me and my chest ached with the trouble I saw in them.

"Jack, something's wrong. Was it me? Do you not like me moving your things?"

Fierceness blazed in Jack's eyes. "No. Fuck no. I don't care about that. You do whatever you need to feel comfortable."

Barely relieved, I nodded. "Then what upset you?"

Jack hesitated, then blurted, "It's this case for work," and the story of the Judge, a serial killer with a penchant for using Bible quotes, tumbled out uncontrolled, until he said, "It's like he believes he's doing a good thing by getting rid of these people he doesn't like," and instantly looked horrified with himself.

Because that was what I'd told him when he asked if I believed what I did was wrong. I broke the law, yes, but given a choice, I only ever did what the law was too restricted to do. Sometimes, it didn't work that way and an innocent person died, but I tried. I truly did.

"He's different from us," Jack said firmly. "Adam says he'd playing God, like it's his *burden* or something."

Adam? Who was Adam? But in the diatribe about feeling as if he had nothing to offer in the investigation into this serial killer that followed, Jack explained that Adam was Dr. Adam Quinn, the profiler on the case. The familiarity of him calling the man "Adam" and not "Dr. Quinn" unsettled me somewhat, but was lost as Jack wound down, sagging against me, head resting desultorily on my shoulder, mumbling apologies for unloading on me.

Absurdly glad he felt he could, and worried that he had to, I wrapped him in my arms, wanting to protect and comfort. "It's all right, Jack. You can trust me. I'll help you any way I can."

I'd even ignore Dejana and the police if I had to. Jack was much more important than any of them.

Not in the mood for sex after his venting, Jack let me take him to bed and we simply lay close until he drifted off. I dozed throughout the night but didn't let myself fall into deep sleep. Jack was restless and I watched over him as he struggled in his dreams, wishing I could do more than brush the black curls off his forehead, or kiss his cheek, or hold him until he quieted. He woke well enough in the morning however, and dragged me into the shower with him, leaving me limp and sated when he returned to the Surry Hills LAC and the hunt for the Judge.

Cautious of igniting more interest from the local police, I decided against working on the Monaro and resigned myself to a day in the apartment. I sent a message to Nine asking if she could find out why the Sydney police were interested in me and got a curse-laden but generally positive response that boiled down to "I'll try, don't hold your breath." Then I unpacked.

There was absolutely no organisational structure to Jack's personal items. I supposed there was a vague demarcation between work and personal clothes in the closet and a general socks and underwear, shirts and shorts, and anything else order to the drawers of the tallboy, but it all overlapped with distressing frequency. With Jack's words—*do whatever you need to feel comfortable*—in mind, I began rearranging, mostly to fit my clothes in alongside his, but to also quiet the buzzing need in my veins for order.

Occasionally I found myself replaying another thing Jack had said—*It's like he believes he's doing a good thing by getting rid of these people he doesn't like*—and wondering if he'd ever felt that disgusted with me.

It was almost a welcome distraction when Dejana's phone vibrated in my back pocket.

"Yes?" As it had the day before, it felt almost peaceful slipping back into the Ethan Blade persona. I knew this. Despite Jack's reassurance, I didn't know the etiquette of rearranging a lover's home.

"Sniper nest, two hours," Dejana said then hung up.

I was in place and secure on the rooftop half an hour early. In the shadow of the stairwell, I snapped the rifle together while keeping an eye on Dejana's office window across the way. The plain white room was empty. From this angle I could see she hid nothing behind her desk. She really did carry everything she needed in her head.

Rifle ready, I set up my position on the edge of the roof, under cover of a light-coloured tarp I'd bought to help me blend into the cement surface. It was hot under my belly and quickly heated up between my back and the tarp, but I could ignore the temperature, focusing on the office through the rifle's scope. Ten minutes after I was in place, Dejana entered the room and sat in her chair behind the desk. She didn't turn to look at me, trusting that I was there.

I shifted focus to the door to the office, making sure I could find it fast. Then down the outside of the building to the front entrance. People came and went, none of them triggering my senses as potential danger. Half an hour past the time Dejana had given me, the door to the office opened and a woman entered. She was dressed in bike leathers, black from neck to toe, though her jacket hung open, showing no concealed weapons. The meeting with Dejana took less than ten minutes, then she left. Eighteen minutes later, the next client appeared.

Five people came to see Dejana at various intervals over the next three hours. Only with one of them did she start to raise her hand in a signal to fire, but lowered it before completing the gesture. Any relief I may have felt vanished the instant I saw her next visitor.

The nearly seven-foot tall frame in a dark blue suit was unmistakable.

Two.

My fellow Cabal assassin. My brother. My torturer.

The crosshairs framed the centre of his chest. A killing shot. Fast. Efficient. Done. The world would be free of one of the most successful and talented assassins. And I'd sleep deeper knowing he would never hurt me again.

Two sat opposite Dejana, an easy smile on his face, long legs stretched out and crossed at the ankles. He knew I was there, though, because when he spoke it was with his head turned so I couldn't read his lips. That didn't mean he wasn't willing to communicate, however.

Ping.

I ignored it. It could have been a message from Nine, with the information I'd requested, but even if it was it was a distraction I couldn't afford.

Ping.

The entire time he chatted with Dejana he continued to *ping* me, and I continued to ignore him while wondering what I would do if she signalled a shot. I wanted to think I would complete the job as required.

Not five minutes after walking into the office, Two stood and buttoned his suit jacket. He nodded to Dejana and left. I wanted to move, to go after him and demand a reason why he was in Sydney now, but Dejana didn't indicate my part was over. I stayed as I was, emotions locked down, as yet another client came in. Even as the door to the stairwell behind me opened and footsteps headed towards my position.

Two didn't need to make any noise as he approached. That he did told me he wasn't here to kill—at least not before he'd amused himself.

"One-three," he said. "How very surprising to find you here."

I focused on the man reaching across the table in the office, pushing a folded piece of paper at Dejana insistently, even though she refused to accept it.

Two moved into my peripheral vision, long, lean legs spread, the swish of material as he pushed his jacket back to put his hands on his hips—to make drawing a weapon easier.

"I believe I heard through the wires you had retired, yet here you are. If you're short of money, little brother, I'm sure we could arrange something more respectable than this."

Dejana's client was getting upset, shifting in his seat and glaring from her to the paper he'd left on the desk, then across the street at Two standing tall and unmissable, clearly watching the meeting. From the client's agitation and the intensity of the looks he was casting our way, Dejana had to know something was going on here, but she was a consummate professional, concentrating on the man in front of her.

Two hitched up his pants and crouched, forearms resting on his knees, empty hands dangling between them. "He'll make his move in thirty seconds. Kick the chair back and dive for Dejana."

I agreed with Two's prediction but didn't acknowledge it, even when it happened almost precisely to the second he said.

Dejana moved fast, pushing herself to the side as he lunged over the desktop. Swiftly, competently, Dejana had the client pinned with a thick heeled shoe against this throat and an arm twisted behind him, almost at the point of popping his shoulder out of the socket.

Still no signal.

Calm as you please, Dejana spoke to the client until he was crying and nodding frantically. When she released him, he curled into a hurting ball for a moment, then fled as fast as he could. Once the door was closed behind him and five minutes had passed, Dejana gave me the "stand-down" signal.

I rolled, flinging the tarp off and twisting to sweep my legs through Two's. He jumped from his crouched position up onto the parapet, escaping my move. As intended. Its true purpose was to give me a precious second to aim the rifle at him.

CHAPTER SEVEN

Two balanced on the raised edge of the roof, lips warped into a vicious snarl, hands reaching for the knives I knew he carried at the base of his spine. My finger was heavy on the rifle's trigger, only the barest extra pressure required to fire. Then Two's face smoothed out and he flashed me a charming smile, familiar and fake, and as always, it ignited a tiny sliver of anxiety in my belly. That smile was a bright, welcoming, deadly trap.

"Why are you here, Two?" My tone was steady and firm.

Slowly, deliberately, Two sat down on the parapet, facing me. "I have a job."

"Australia isn't your territory."

He smirked. "It isn't yours either, yet here *you* are."

Keeping the rifle trained on Two, I got to my feet, stepping clear of the tarp. "Why isn't Seven on the job?"

Two stood with me, moving in the opposite direction, keeping the distance between us. He didn't lose the smile. "She's . . . sitting this one out. After the mess you left her with in Vietnam, I thought I'd help her."

Normally, I had absolutely no reason to fear for my sister, but Two was different to any other threat Seven could ever face.

"Then do the job and leave." I resettled the rifle in my grip.

"You have my word." Two put his right hand over his heart, but his tone was mocking. Then his whole body shifted slightly. Just enough to put me on alert for an imminent attack. "I know why you're here." His voice had lowered and lost the sardonic inflection. "For the spy."

Not showing him any reaction, I moved again and he moved with me until we were circling slowly.

"The target who should be dead," Two continued. "The one you failed to kill, and then stopped me from killing in your place, One-three." He ceased mirroring me and came forwards, slow but pointed. "I know now why you didn't kill him. Why you submitted to the punishment. You . . ." Expression flicking through disgust, he spat out, "You bedded him. Tell me truthfully, brother, is he that good?" Mood as mercurial as always, Two suddenly looked concerned. "Do you think you're *normal* enough for him?"

I would not talk about Jack with Two. Would not taint what we had by bringing it any closer to my past. To the one person who, more so than any of the sadists the Cabal gave us to as children, had turned my childhood into a bloody mess.

"You promise you will leave as soon as your job is done?"

Two kept advancing. "For you, brother, anything." The smile came back, so like the one that had drawn me to him all those years ago, when I was scared and lost and I believed he was kind. "Anything," he whispered and he was right there, at the very end of the rifle, chest a mere inch from the silencer.

I locked away all the chaos his appearance here in Sydney caused, and met the dark panes of his sunglasses unflinchingly. "Good."

Two grabbed the silencer and wrenched the barrel of the rifle aside. I let it go without a fight. For a second, Two was unbalanced. My opening.

I stepped into him, one, two, punches to his abdomen. Spinning, I slammed an elbow into his side. Two grunted and one of his long arms snapped around my neck. I pushed back before he could tighten his hold, turning enough to hook a foot behind his leg. When he clamped his forearm over my throat and pulled, I yanked his leg forward and down he went. Taking me with him.

The fall broke his hold and I rolled away and to my feet, ready for the next attack.

Two flipped to his feet and came at me. I backed up, deflecting his kicks and punches, looking for another opening to get inside his reach.

"Come, One-three." He feinted a punch with his right hand then tried to land a kick on my ribs. I danced out of the way as he said, "Why the hostility? You know I don't want to hurt you."

He may believe he didn't *want* to, and yet found it *necessary* with disturbing frequency. I was older now. I knew his patterns and wouldn't fall for his supposed sincerity anymore.

"You've made a mistake, that's all," he continued, a pleading note in his voice, even as he launched a fast combination of strikes I ducked and deflected. "Forget the spy. Come home with me."

"No."

I launched into a spinning kick and knocked Two backwards several paces. Followed it with a leap and knee to his chest. He staggered backwards and his calves hit the low parapet, arms pinwheeling for balance. Another blow would send him over the edge.

Backing off, I flexed my hands out of the fists they'd curled into.

Two, realising his display of ineptitude had failed to draw me close, stilled. "You always were too stubborn, One-three." With a flick of his wrist, a knife appeared in his hand, then he came at me again.

He was a fraction too fast, and I moved to meet him, getting inside his space. I grabbed his knife arm, wrenched it down and, using my whole body to block and lift, tossed him over my back. Two hit the cement hard, but he rolled and came up on his feet, blade still in hand.

I popped one of my own knives from its sheath and we clashed again. I blocked his weapon high and drove mine towards his belly. Two dropped his knife, caught it in his free hand and slashed at my arm. I pulled my blow, disengaging, but he caught my high hand before I got away.

Two's mouth curled into a snarl and he twisted my wrist, aiming to break. I went with the sharp turn, flipping my entire body. It broke his hold but I came down badly. My knife skittered away when I hit the hard ground on one knee, reaching out to steady myself. Long legs covering the distance between us in a single step, Two got a hand around my throat and hauled me upright. Other hand around my upper arm, he lifted me off the ground and in another long stride, slammed me against the side of the stairwell entrance. Something hard jabbed into my shoulder blade.

Fingers tight but not damaging around my neck, Two leaned in close so he could whisper directly into my ear.

"You'll come home with me, little brother. One way or another."

"Never," I choked out.

"We'll see." He pulled back and his smile was soft and tender. "You could never stay away for long. You always come back to me . . . Paul."

Air caught in my lungs, frozen and sharp. That name—*my* name— from his tongue scared me. None of the others ever used it, and if they ever did, they would never infuse it with the levels of intimacy and threat Two did.

Two let go of me and took several long steps back, straightening his suit. I slumped against the wall, dragging warm air into my lungs, trying to melt the shards of ice Two left in there.

"This has been pleasant, One-three. Maybe our paths will cross again." With consummate arrogance, he turned his back on me and picked up the knife he'd dropped.

I rolled my shoulder, pain sharpening and spreading. "Finish your job and leave."

Tucking his knife away, Two threw me another smile and headed for the stairwell door. "That's the plan." Then he was gone.

I could've lied and said the time I spent leaning on the wall was to ensure Two wasn't waiting inside to ambush me, and it was partially. It did, however, give me a few moments to catch my breath and settle my nerves.

When I was certain he was gone, and my hands were steady, I cleaned up the sniper nest, hiding my equipment in a vent opening. As I finished, Dejana's phone vibrated. Rather surprised it had survived the altercation with Two, I answered it.

"Ensure nothing like that happens again while you're on my clock. You're done for the day," she said and hung up.

By the time I made it back to Leichhardt, it was past sundown and yet Jack wasn't home. I put away the groceries I'd bought—having food delivered constantly made me anxious—showered, iced my shoulder, and finished organising the clothes. And still Jack wasn't home. I did some upgrades on the security system, making the sensors more sensitive and widening the range of the external cameras. That done, I went to bed, alone.

Jack came in not long later, crawling into bed and whispering his desires, hands imploring me to turn over for him.

The aches from the fight had set in when I stopped moving and I still felt rattled by Two's proximity. "In the morning, Jack."

He took it gracefully, settling down behind me, snuggled in close and was asleep in moments.

I ended up falling asleep around two a.m. but not so deeply Jack couldn't wake me with a few well-placed kisses in the morning. This time, I rolled over and the sex was slow and tender, grounding me back in the life we were making together. Though the peace was dinted when Jack found the bruise on my shoulder blade in the shower. It did, however, lead to a scalp massage and blowjob that helped me through what could have been a disastrous breakfast.

"You reorganised the closet and tallboy."

His tone was light, but so soon after an encounter with Two, I almost distrusted it. "I can change it back if it's not all right."

Worry flittered through Jack's eyes for a moment, then he gripped the back of my neck, fingers pushing into my hair. Familiar, affectionate, caring. I resisted but couldn't win the fight and relaxed into the touch, wanting the love I hoped it conveyed.

"It's perfect. Exactly what I wanted."

Eyebrow arching, I asked, "Exactly?"

Jack pulled my head back. "Exactly." And he kissed up my neck, leaving his coffee scent on my skin. I didn't entirely mind. "Don't you have a job to get to?"

"Eventually." A couple more biting kisses, then Jack let me go and explained his plan for a demonstration at the LAC.

Pleased his grumbles about being undercover again seemed to be less, I let domestic issues consume me through breakfast. The simple pleasantness of it let me spill one of my deeper secrets when Jack asked about my reaction to him touching my head.

"I don't recall much from my early childhood. I believe I told you once I was blind until I was six, or thereabouts." Jack's nod and silence didn't sound alarms in my head, so I continued. "As such, I have no memories of my mother's face. I have a vague memory of her singing. At least, I think it's her. It's a lullaby, so I choose to believe it was she who sang it to me. By far the strongest memory I have is her running her hand through my hair. Sometimes it was to comfort me. Sometimes to comfort her."

My memories of that time were chaotic. Some I couldn't tell if they were from my time with my mother, or the first several months with the group of Sugar Babies who would become my "family." The touches to my head and hair, though, they *were* my mother. They had to be. No one in the other place ever had a kind touch. That was perhaps why I clung so hard to those few memories I had of the woman who'd birthed me, claimed she loved me, and abandoned me.

Jack's expression was studiously neutral. It was one I had become very familiar with over the past year. First it had been common when he'd been trying to not show his anger or frustration with me. More and more often, however, it appeared when he was feeling those things on my behalf, directed at those he perceived as a threat to me, physically or emotionally. I hated that I was the reason he felt that pain and rage, but it was also a relief. If Jack felt that way, then it was all right I did as well. It gave me hope that he wouldn't reject me for all the things he didn't yet know.

Perhaps I could give him something more. Correct a lie of omission and see how he reacted.

"Sometimes, it was neither of those things. Those times, she would stroke my head as I was falling asleep, and say, Paul, ma petite erreur."

Jack had made it clear that he believed my accent made me British. It was a common misconception I relied on, but one I didn't want to need with Jack anymore.

The longer Jack remained silent the more I began doubt telling him I was French, not English. Compared to most of the lies I'd told him, this might not have seemed important, but it was to me. This one tiny morsel of my past was something I'd clung to, desperately at times, during the years with the group. Knowing where I'd come from meant I wasn't what the Cabal was trying to make me into. It meant I wasn't like the other children who hurt me because they didn't know any better. It meant I was still Paul St. Clair, even if Paul had to become a ghost for One-three to survive and escape.

And yet, if Jack reacted as if it was anything other than a passing curiosity I felt I might scramble like an army was on my tail. I wanted him to know, but I didn't want to talk about it either.

"What was the lullaby?"

I fought down the urge to tell him he was perfect. It would only go to his handsome head.

"I don't remember all of it, but it was about a chicken. A grey one, or a brown one. Or perhaps there were many chickens. Either way, it or they laid eggs in very unusual places and a little boy would eat the eggs while they were still warm."

"Warm from the chicken's bum or from being cooked?"

Trust Jack to get to the real heart of any issue.

In that moment I made a decision, so while Jack tidied the kitchen, I suited up and met him on the way to the bathroom to brush teeth.

Jack tugged on the back of my collar. "Those look like going-out clothes."

"I have a meeting today."

"With your banker?" Jack smirked, but he didn't know how close to the truth he was.

"Not exactly."

Jack bugged me about it all the way out of the apartment, only stopping when we ran into Rocco and Short Round. The dachshund clambered at my legs so I reacquainted myself with the lively dog while the others talked. Rocco remembered me from the start of the year and complimented Victoria, while Jack pretended to grumble about us maligning his poor old Kawasaki Ninja, which we did not do, directly.

Then Jack's hand landed on my lower back. "Don't you have your mysterious appointment to get to? And I can't be much later than I already am."

The reaction to move away from the touch was instinctual. I needed complete control when I wasn't in a safe place, to be ready and prepared to fight for my life. For Jack's life. For Rocco's and Shorty's lives. Anyone touching me—*Jack* touching me—would delay my reactions, perhaps fatally.

Jack kept his hands to himself as we said our goodbyes and all the way down to the garage. When I turned to wish him a good day at work, I saw just how unhappy he was. It wasn't the first time I'd brushed off his hold in public, but our relationship had still been somewhat questionable those times, whereas this time, it really appeared to effect him.

"Jack?"

He surveilled the garage, then relaxed fractionally. "You seem to be settling in okay."

"I'm not completely socially inept, Jack."

"I never said you were."

"Then what has you worried?"

"You. I know you're not used to this sort of exposure."

Was he worried how I, a killer like the Judge, would cope with this sort of life?

Instantly ashamed of the thought—Jack was disgusted by the Judge's motives, not *mine*—I still couldn't quite shake it when I said, "You don't know what I'm used to, Jack."

"True." Though he didn't appear to enjoy saying it. "So, this is normal for you? Living with another man. Being seen in public with him as a gay couple. That's just everyday for you, is it?" Jack paused to pull in a breath, his gaze boring into me as if he could slice away my skin and see the mess within. "Mr. Cesare's cool. He tried to set me up with one of his grandsons once. But not everyone is like him. Most people don't care, but those that do tend to really *not* like seeing two men together."

"I'm aware of that."

"Being aware of it is one thing. Being the subject of it is something else. I *know* you've never done this before. Have a relationship with someone. Live with them like this. Unless you were lying about that, too."

Lying about that? I shook my head firmly. Everything else, though . . .

"*That's* what I'm worried about. How you'll feel knowing people don't like you being with me."

CHAPTER EIGHT

Jack's concern was valid. I hadn't been in a relationship before, let alone a homosexual one which came with added hazards. Physical altercations were not an issue and I had been called enough names in my life—freak, mutant, bad luck, psychopath—that slurs directed at me had little power. I didn't care about people in general knowing I was with another man.

I did care that I was back to lying to Jack about so many things, however. He didn't deserve that from me after everything I'd put him through over the past two years.

"Jack, I'm sorry. I didn't mean to worry you. You're right. I don't have experience with any of those things, and I can't promise that I won't make mistakes upon occasion. I can, however, assure you that regardless of what anyone else thinks or says, I want to be here. With you." All the things I really wanted to apologise for, but couldn't admit to yet, hovered just under my words and I hoped he heard that.

Jack came closer. "I want you here, too. It's why I asked you to come and stay. I know it's not going to be easy. I don't have a great track record with relationships. *I'm* undoubtedly going to mess something up at some stage."

A tension I hadn't been aware of in my chest eased. Jack was as uncertain as I was? It shouldn't, but knowing that made me smile. "We're not incapable men, Jack. I'm sure we can weather the rough patches. And if you were to leave me, I should remind you, I'm retired, not disabled."

Jack snorted and took another step towards me. I backed up, as I had in the corridor. Instincts didn't change as easily as minds.

"Too soon?" I hoped to deflect him from pushing my limits again.

It stopped him with barely a foot between us. "Too cheesy," he corrected in a smoky rumble.

"Jack, am I required to remind you we're not exactly in private?" Although lust seemed to suppress my instincts so well it frightened me.

After a charged moment, Jack backed off. "No. Just wanted to tell you that I'll miss you today."

My hand was on his chest without thought. I needed to feel him, to reassure him, and myself. To let us both know that I wanted to be different, to be better. "And I you."

Jack smiled and I returned it effortlessly. Making him smile never stopped thrilling me. Leaving him happy made it easier for me to go.

I met Brian Steinhauer at the building on Bathurst Street. He greeted me with a wide smile and firm handshake.

"Mr. Sinclair," he said. "It's good to finally meet you face to face. I had started to worry we wouldn't hear from you again."

"I'm sorry for the silence, but there were unavoidable delays overseas," I said in my usual British accent, then gestured at the new building. "Construction appears complete."

The agent went into an extended sales pitch even though I'd finalised the papers on the penthouse midyear. As he recited all the features of the building and its prime location, I kept an eye out for anyone lurking about. It was impossible to hide completely from the Cabal, especially when they knew I had a strong interest in Sydney, but I would do everything I could to keep everyone else from finding this safe place.

Finally, Brian gestured me into the building ahead of him and we discussed the general security they had installed. It was impressive for a residential structure, but nowhere near my requirements. It would be a relatively simple thing to tap into their system and add to it, though.

We moved on to the private lift to the penthouse. Brian gave me the security code, a simple four-digit number I would be changing as soon as he left. Before swapping it out entirely for my own device.

The entryway to the penthouse had been decorated as the foyer downstairs but I would have the potted plants removed and take the mirrored walls back to brick. The fewer potential weapons and obstacles the better if I had to fight my way in, or out. At least the reinforced steel door I'd ordered had been installed. Inside was bare. Polished wood floors and walls painted the pale champagne I'd picked out. A blank canvass. One I'd hoped Jack would be a part of filling up, but after everything that had led up to Canberra, I hadn't been sure. Now I wanted to finish it alone and pinned my hopes on Jack loving the surprise.

Brian insisted on a tour of the place, since it was my first time seeing it. I'd bought it off the blueprint before the building had been completed, which had allowed me to add a few extras to the construction. We signed the final bits of paperwork on the kitchen countertop, admired the view of Hyde Park and the cathedral, then I shooed Brian out.

My first order of business was to change all the security codes, then I retrieved Victoria and parked her in the underground garage. With a bag of tools and another of my own security devices, I went back to the penthouse, removed my jacket, rolled up my sleeves and got to work.

By the time I felt hunger pangs, the place was no longer pristine. There was sawdust, cement chips, broken plaster and dangling wires everywhere. It was a mess, but I felt good about it. I was working towards a solid future with Jack.

Ping.

I hesitated to answer, in case it was Two, but I couldn't hide from him forever.

"I sure hope I'm not interrupting something super special," Nine drawled.

"You're not," I assured her firmly.

"Really? So you're not all sweaty and naked?"

Frowning, I fetched the button-down I'd removed when I got too hot and shrugged it back on. "No."

Her laugh said she didn't believe me.

"I assume you have some information for me?"

Nine's amusement didn't entirely abate, her words coming through with a tremble of laughter in them. *"You're not going to like it."*

"Just tell me. Why are the police interested in me?"

"They're not. At least not that I can find and most police departments aren't hard to crack. Besides, I got Seven onto it and she knows all the tricks." The humour disappeared in the bitterness of many old injuries, real and perceived ones. *"She said there is nothing that even hints at you, either local, state or federal. Every mention of Ethan Blade has been cleaned up by the Office and any new inquiries get knocked down very quickly."*

At least Director Tan was keeping up his part of the agreement he and Jack had struck. But it didn't explain why a police officer had been asking questions about me at the garage complex.

"Did you know Two was in Sydney?" I asked.

There was silence for a long moment, then Nine said slowly, *"No. How do you know he is?"*

I snorted. "He found me, of course."

"Not surprised. He always did have perfect One-three-radar."

Ignoring that, I said, "He claims he's here on a job. Did Seven mention it to you?"

"Because we chatted about our lives and periods and which garrotte we prefer to use, sure. No, you weirdo, she didn't mention it. Didn't you ask him?"

"He said he was doing a favour for Seven."

Nine laughed. *"Right, 'cause they're such great friends."* The hilarity died instantly and, grimly, she said, *"You know why he's there."*

Her words sparked that same sense of anxiety in me that Two's presence did. "Yes."

Deadly serious, Nine said, *"Be careful, One-three. Watch him, don't let him close with you."*

It was good advice, and not just during a fight with Two. He didn't need to be punching a person in order to hurt them.

"I'm not about to invite him in for tea." My tone was perhaps a bit testier than it should have been.

"You could have fooled me." Something like tenderness might have tinged her voice. *"You're not exactly rational where he's concerned, you know. Things get . . . messy between you."*

I blinked away the stinging in my eyes. "Not anymore. I won't let him get to me."

"You better not." Then, in a brighter tone, she added, *"Your cooking is getting better and I've decided you can practice anytime we're in the same place."*

"Very generous of you." Nine would eat food burned beyond recognition when she was hungry enough, which was a rather consistent state with her.

"I know. If Seven ever answers a message from me, I'll ask her about the job."

"Thank you. I'll send her a message as well. The more information I have the better."

"Just don't let him close with you," she reiterated, then the connection was cut.

I sat for a while afterwards, considering the new intelligence. Had it been pure happenstance that an officer described someone who looked like me? There was an outside chance it was related to Jack's current job, as he was working with the Sydney police and I was apparently similar enough to a serial killer Jack had made connections between myself and the Judge.

Seven didn't answer when I *ping*ed her, which wasn't unusual, so I left a message and then contemplated the penthouse. I'd completely rewired the security system and fitted my custom-made number pads. All codes had been changed and it was as close to secure as it could be.

Leaving Bathurst Street, I returned to Leichhardt, showered, and waited for Jack.

In the days that followed, neither myself nor Nine heard back from Seven—mildly worrying but not alarming as she often went quiet—and I fell into a routine. Nights and mornings with Jack, the days spent alternating between working on the penthouse and Monaro and sitting watch over Dejana's meetings. The former tasks were rewarding pass-times, the latter not so much. Until the day it went from tedium to excitement rather fast.

Dejana was talking with Grant Owen again. He had, wisely, left his family elsewhere this day when we joined him at the Centennial Park Labyrinth, a cement circle with a pattern marked on it. The area around it was perhaps a hundred square meters of open grass bordered by trees to the north and west and two ponds to the east and south. Geese and black swans paddled across the water peacefully.

Today's meeting wasn't as calm as the first one. The young politician was agitated and while I held back far enough to not overhear anything, his voice rose enough every now and then that I caught snippets of words. Including the current prime minister's name and at one particularly heated moment, "worst military loss in recent history." Dejana shushed him with a single wave of a hand and kept her voice low and calm, settling him down.

Movement in the trees to the west caught my eye. Even before I fully registered it, I took two long strides and launched myself at Dejana and Owen. "Down!" I commanded even as I swept them over with my arms. They went down to either side of me and I hit the cement of the labyrinth on my side, the crack of my hip on the hard surface louder than that of the silenced shot from the tree line.

"Stay down," I instructed, then rolled over, tracking the shooter with my Desert Eagle.

The shadowed figure darted back into deeper cover, heading towards the remains of the swamp that once covered the entire park area.

I quickly scanned the rest of the tree line and found no other signs of hostiles. "Looks clear," I reported to Dejana.

"Then go." If she was rattled at all she gave no indication. "Make sure they don't get a second chance at us."

As I ran into the trees, I switched out the Eagle for the silenced Glock. This part of the park wasn't heavily trafficked after the morning tai chi class finished, but it wasn't entirely empty of innocent bystanders. Thankfully none of them were taking a stroll on the wooden walkway in the Lachlan Swamp, and from the lack of footsteps on the hollow boards, neither was the shooter.

Tall, scraggly paperbarks spread away to either side of the pathway, the long-bladed grass between them almost as tall as I was. Anyone rushing through it would create enough noise to pinpoint them. The swamp was silent.

"Damn it," I muttered and jogged back the way I'd come.

I didn't go far, instead sliding in behind a large tree trunk a couple dozen yards away and waiting. The shooter certainly wasn't a patient sort, leaving their hiding spot amongst the long grass within a couple of minutes. I listened carefully to the rustle of the plants, to the soft tread of their shoes, judging distance and direction. Then I moved.

The shooter was creeping out of the paperbarks, scanning the direction I'd retreated, their gun at the ready. They still weren't fast enough.

My bullet caught them in the right shoulder, knocking them back and sending the gun flying from their hand. With a startled yelp, they held their injured arm close and, this time uncaring of the noise, jumped up onto the wooden path and ran.

I followed. The hip I'd hit the cement on gave out little bursts of fire with each step, but it was easily ignored. The pound of our heavy feet was loud but I still heard the shooter's pained gasps, even when I lost sight of their forest-camouflaged body around a curve in the path. I also heard the surprised cry that was cut off very abruptly.

Skidding to a stop before moving around the curve, I listened carefully and heard the heavy thump of a body hitting the wooden planks.

"It's all right, One-three. I took care of it for you."

Two.

I should have expected he'd reappear at some point. It would have been impossible for him to leave the country without a final visit. That hope gave me the steadiness to walk around the curve, still cautious and gun at the ready, however.

The shooter lay on the planks of the boardwalk, sprawled in an ungainly tumble of limbs that said they wouldn't be walking away from this. Sightless eyes stared at me through the holes in their dark green balaclava. Two stood over them, arms crossed and satisfied smirk on his face.

"My gift to you, little brother," he said.

"What if I'd required them alive?"

Two shrugged. "He was a hired goon pretending to be an *assassin*. What could he have known, apart from the target's face?"

"Precisely. The target. Who hired him. Why that target."

"Oh, dear. Has the spy recruited you to the cause?" Two chuckled. "Poor One-three. You always did latch on to anyone who showed you even the barest hint of kindness."

Doing my best to ignore his barbs, I crouched by the shooter and patted the body down. He certainly hadn't been a professional assassin of the class I was used to encountering. Perhaps he had been silly enough to keep information about the job upon his person.

Two squatted opposite me, watching keenly. He wore dark pants and what appeared to be a white undershirt, as if he'd ditched a recognisable part of his clothes.

"I thought you were leaving when your job was done." I went through the pants pockets on the body.

"I will. When it's done."

Hiding my shock, I said, "You don't usually take so long on a job." Generally because Two didn't bother with proof that his target required killing. He found them, killed them, left the body and never considered them again. I sometimes believed he didn't consider them as human. To him, they were only targets. We were all targets.

"I'm taking a leaf from your book."

The shooter had been smart enough to not bring anything incriminating with him at least. Which gave me nothing to do but look at Two enquiringly. "What do you mean?"

Two's smile was a little shy. "I've made a plan, One-three. I'm making sure I have the right target. Making sure he's guilty."

"That's good," I murmured even as I wondered where the trap was. If Two was being this reasonable, then he was hiding a knife somewhere, waiting to strike. "You shouldn't trust the Cabal implicitly."

"Oh, I don't. At least, not on this matter."

We stood at the same time, not once taking our gaze off the other. I kept the Glock in hand, while Two was empty handed, which didn't diminish his threat level in the least. Tension strummed through my muscles, trying to anticipate where the attack would come from.

"See you soon, little brother." Two turned and walked away, casual and relaxed.

I watched until he was out of sight, then waited another ten minutes. He didn't come back, either openly or stealthily. Accepting that there would be no fight this time, I pushed the body off the boardwalk and jogged back to where I'd left Dejana. She had moved Owen into the cover of the trees, standing with their backs to trunks opposite each other, so they could cover all approaches. Owen squeaked in surprise when I appeared silently from behind him. Dejana had seen me coming but hadn't warned him.

I escorted them out of the park and into their respective cars, then called a taxi for myself. I went straight to Leichhardt, wanting the security of home more than anything else right then.

CHAPTER NINE

I didn't find the serenity I needed at home, however. Jack had put our boxer-briefs in the T-shirt drawer of the tallboy and before I knew it, all the clothes were on the floor of the bedroom and I was folding and refolding everything at least twice before putting it back where it belonged. Jack didn't mean anything by it. He was just a bit careless or didn't understand. That was all. It wasn't malicious. He just didn't understand.

Why didn't he understand?

There was so much chaos in the world that couldn't be controlled, but this was something I could keep ordered. Was that so hard to fathom? Was it too much to ask of him? It was just one small matter in the great messy scheme of things and it wouldn't hurt him to just accept that this was the only way to store our clothes.

At least when Jack came home, earlier than usual for him lately, he didn't push the matter and left me alone. He kept to the living room, trying to be unobtrusive, yet I could feel him out there, pacing, wondering, questioning. So I ran through argument after argument in my head about why this was important. About why unpredictability was a danger we had to avoid whenever we could.

I couldn't eat dinner and I don't think Jack did either, but we did go to bed together. Jack kept to himself and I lay beside him, unable to sleep, listening to his snores, and thought perhaps this wasn't going to work. We were clearly worlds apart, and maybe he felt my need for order was just another tick in the serial killer column.

It was illogical. Jack couldn't think I was anything like a serial killer. He wouldn't have wanted to continue seeing me if he did. And yet he had to have made the connection on some level to bring it up.

For as long as I'd been aware of what the Cabal had tried to turn me into, I had fought them. I hadn't won all of the time, but I'd gotten to a point where I could live with it, and myself. I only killed when the target deserved it. I killed for the right reasons . . . just as the Judge believed they did.

My thoughts spiralled around the same arguments, keeping me awake and half convinced Jack couldn't really want me. Then he rolled over in his sleep and wound around me, face smashed mostly into my armpit. I had lost count of the number times this had happened over the past year. Usually after we'd spent hours having sex and messing around. This was one of Jack's affections that always disarmed and charmed me, his unconscious need to hold me close.

This meant more than a thoughtless comment said in a tired rant.

I still didn't sleep but at least my head wasn't clogged with dark thoughts. Turning into Jack, I held him back.

By the time Jack awoke, I felt more ordered. He was wary still, for which I was grateful. One kind touch or overly caring word would knock me off balance again and Jack seemed to pick up on that. Though he did hesitate at the door, helmet under his arm. It had become a ritual of sorts, if I was awake when he left, that he gave me one of a variety of kisses to my cheek on his way out.

"I'll be here tonight," I promised him.

Jack smiled. "Good. I'll miss you." Then he left.

I needed a day of quiet and peace, so I worked on the Monaro. She was coming along very well as sourcing genuine parts was easy with my car-thief contact three doors down in the complex. Ken came by to mention another visit by the same police officer as before. I thanked him and asked him to call me if the officer appeared again. Without an official case, following the cop was my only recourse to find out what it was about.

A couple of days later, Rocco caught up to me in the garage at home and broached the subject of a security system for his apartment.

"Shorty's been a bit nervous lately," he explained as I cradled the dachshund in my arms on the way upstairs. "He barks at people passing in the hallway more than usual, and I could barely get him out of the apartment this morning for our walk."

Not liking the pattern Rocco was innocently describing, I assured him I would have them safe and sound within a couple of days. I spent the afternoon measuring his place for sensors and cameras. Of course Jack found me there and his eyes lit up with barely restrained lust as he wolf whistled. We hadn't had sex since before the underwear incident, and my cock responded so fast to Jack's expression I nearly jumped him then and there.

Gaze locked onto my toolbelt, he asked, "What are you doing?"

"Rocco asked if I'd look at installing an alarm system for him."

"And you actually are?"

"I don't see why I shouldn't. He's a lovely gentleman, and I don't mind helping him. Don't worry, I'm only charging him for the cost of the system."

As if on cue, Rocco returned with the drink he'd offered me. "Your drink, son."

I took the iced tea with a warm rush of fondness. I'd decided I liked this man calling me "son."

"Hello, Nishant." Rocco used Jack's Indian middle name. "I hope you don't mind, but I stole your young man today for my own purposes."

"It's all good, Mr. Cesare. Just check his pockets before he leaves. I fear I'm going to find Shorty held hostage in our place soon."

Rocco said something and left and Shorty made a fuss at our feet. All of it faded into the background as I stared at Jack.

"What?" The word was warily amused.

"You said 'our place.'" Two small words but they reverberated in my head like bullets ricocheting in a closed space.

"Yeah. Is that okay?"

Words abandoned me. I nodded.

"Good. You going to be much longer here?"

"I have a few more measurements to get, but that won't take long."

Jack started walking towards our apartment. "I'll be waiting for you, then. Oh, and when you come in, leave the toolbelt on."

I had to remind myself over and over that I'd promised to help Rocco and Shorty as I got the final numbers down. I did, however, leave without finishing the tea Rocco brought me.

Inside the apartment, I found a trail of Jack's clothes leading from the door to the bedroom—his riding gloves, tie, belt, a single sock. Just a few items to lead me to him, naked on the bed, lying back against a pile of pillows, the fingers of one hand trailing idly up and down his hard cock. I stalled in the doorway, breathless and entranced. Mostly by the beautiful body waiting for me, but partly because the majority of Jack's clothes were in the laundry basket.

"Thank you." I barely had the air to give the words sound.

"Anything for you."

I tossed the items I'd gathered in the general direction of the basket and prepared to throw myself at him. Jack sat up and stopped me at the end of the bed. Sitting, he positioned me between his legs and just touched. Fingers skimmed over my thighs and arse, waist and groin, the briefest of brushes before moving on to trace the shapes of the tools hanging in the toolbelt.

"This is hot," Jack murmured. "Never had a handyman fetish before. Pretty sure it's going to stick around, though." He tugged on the leather and moaned when the belt pulled the waistband of my jeans down, exposing a strip of skin from hip to hip and the top of my pubic hair. "Fuck." His fingers traced it slowly.

"Jack." I carded my fingers through his curls. He was setting nerves afire with the lightest of pressure. With the pure desire in his voice and eyes.

Slowly, ever so slowly, Jack moved his hands upwards, dragging the T-shirt up. "I got this shirt when I lived in Canberra for officer training. It was a joke from some guys in my course. They overheard a call from my sister, giving me her yearly reminder of what she thought of my life choices."

As he pushed it up, I watched the image of Parliament House disappear, as did the slogan, "You will never find a more wretched hive of scum and villainy." When I'd found it at the bottom of the drawer, I hadn't gotten the reference but thought it amusing all the same. I had been unable to not put it on, imaging this very moment as I did so. "Do you mind me wearing it?"

Jack pressed his face into my bare belly and breathed in deep. "Hell no. If I didn't have to take some clothes off you to fuck you, I wouldn't."

In the end, the T-shirt stayed on the longest. The jeans went first, then the toolbelt when it proved too cumbersome in the positions Jack put me in. But even the shirt was cast aside when Jack needed to "see me" while he drove into me with a fierce passion that left me utterly wrecked.

When the muscles in my legs solidified enough to allow for walking, I staggered into the bathroom to clean up. Coming back with a towel around my waist, I discovered Jack in the kitchen, wearing only shorts and an apron to protect his chest. I'd noticed the chicken pieces marinating that morning, but even so, I nearly skipped when I saw the curry ingredients out on the countertop.

"You look like a kid on his birthday," Jack muttered, smiling. "This isn't that special."

I leaned against his broad, bare back and rested my hands on his biceps as they flexed and bulged. "I have to disagree. If I had a birthday, I would be very satisfied with this."

Jack froze for a second, then slid the chicken pieces into the hot pan. "What do you mean, if you had a birthday?"

Tucking my face against his tattoo, I found the courage to speak. The lullaby discussion had gone down rather well, after all.

"I don't know my birthday. I don't recall it ever being celebrated while I was with my mother, and afterwards . . . That wasn't the sort of thing they cared about. I suppose it's not something I've thought about since. No need to."

For a long while the sizzle of the meat was the only sound. I stayed where I was, wanting the warmth and closeness, and breathed deep of Jack's scent and the heady aroma of the marinade. This was home.

"You need a birthday," Jack eventually said, stirring the curry.

"I've lasted this long without one."

"Yeah, but you didn't have me around to want to make it special for you."

He sounded almost flippant, but the words touched me deeply. I could find no response worthy of the simple yet profound statement. So I kissed his tattoo and stepped back, needing a clear space to fully absorb it.

Jack looked over his shoulder at me, brows pinched together, but smoothing out when he saw my face. "Pick a date." He winked and turned back to the cook top. "I'll take you out to dinner and a movie."

I loved him.

As easy as that I knew it. There were no doubts about if I knew what it felt like, no wondering if I could even fall in love. This wild, crazy, frightening jumble of emotions and physiological oddities couldn't be anything other than love. Otherwise I would have been terrified of them and I wasn't. Almost everything else about this relationship scared me, but not that.

"Jack."

"Yeah? Got a date already?"

"Jack."

Another look over his shoulder, which made him turn around and reach for me. "You okay? Did I say something wrong?"

I wound my arms around his neck and held him tight. My heart was thumping wildly and he must have felt it because he wrapped me up like he was protecting me from an explosion. One hand went to my head, stroking my hair, and I melted.

"Hey," he whispered. "You're scaring me. Ethan, what's wrong?"

"Nothing. Nothing at all."

"You sure?"

"Yes, I'm sure." I sighed and relaxed my hold a fraction. "I just need you to know that—"

"Ow! Shit! Move, move." Jack pushed me against the opposite counter, all but dancing on the spot.

"Jack?"

He spun and reached out to take the boiling curry off the heat. His back was splattered with spots of creamy sauce.

It was a few moments of dashing about to save the butter chicken but in the end, there was little damage to either the dinner or Jack's skin. He cooked the rice while I cleaned up his back, assuring him the tiny red marks would fade by morning.

He smacked my arse playfully. "Go put some pants on at least. Wouldn't want anything delicate getting in harm's way."

Taking the reprieve, I muttered, "We need to talk about this penchant for smacking you've developed."

"Oh, do we, old bean?" he asked in his mocking British accent.

Two could play that game. "Bloody oath, cobber."

Jack cracked up but still somehow managed to grab my towel and yank it off before I got out of range. His laughter dried up in an instant.

"What is that?" He pointed to the fading bruise on my right hip.

"Just an old bump. It's fine now."

"Come here." Jack didn't wait for me to obey but caught up to me and studied the discoloured patch.

It was on the posterior of my hip, spreading over the top of my check. He'd taken me on my back earlier and had apparently missed it then.

"This was more than a bump. What happened?"

"I slipped during tai chi."

He looked into my eyes and after a moment, nodded. "Okay. Do we need to get some matts?"

"No. It was a stupid mistake. I won't make it again."

I loved him and I was lying to him.

Despite the ups and downs proceeding it, dinner was good. The butter chicken tasted just as perfect as always and Jack's mood was wonderfully light and teasing, buoying me along with it. He did raise an eyebrow when I refused seconds, but rapidly decided he didn't care when I took him to the couch and divested him of his shorts.

"Again?" he asked as I stripped off my own and straddled his lap.

"Again," I confirmed, hand wrapped around us both and stroking.

"Jesus," Jack whispered. "How did I get so lucky?"

That nearly derailed the whole thing, but he kissed my throat and all thoughts of confessing everything vanished in a wave of heat. His hands roamed all over me, from knees to thighs, across my flanks, tracing ribs, over my shoulders and down my back to grip my arse and pull me closer. All the while, Jack murmured his desire into my skin with lips, tongue and teeth.

We were both rock hard within moments and I couldn't wait.

Jack laughed when I retrieved the lube I'd stashed in the cushions earlier. "Always prepared."

"One of us must be," I chided as I coated his cock and then shifted over him. His hands spread me wide, fingers grazing my hole, nodding against my chest as I guided his cock into me.

I took him in slow and deep, glorying in the pressure, in the feeling of fullness, of completion. Jack groaned and pushed up as much as he could.

"Fuck. So good."

Agreeing with a frantic nod, I rolled my hips. Both of us moaned loudly as his cock found my prostate. I did it again, and again, and Jack started reciting every swear word he knew, in English, Hindi and what may have been Thai.

"Language, Jack."

His laugh choked off into a strangled gasp as I rose up and slid back down until he was buried to the hilt. "Do that again."

So I did and the swearing started up again. I alternated between thrusting, rolling and simply grinding down as hard as I could. I needed to feel him as deep as possible, wanted to be able to feel him when we weren't together. My cock rubbed over his ridged abdomen, slicking it with pre-come. Jack held his hand over it, keeping it firmly against him. He didn't squeeze or stroke or tease, just made sure I got the friction of his flesh.

I wanted to kiss him. So much. Everything else he gave me so willingly and so often, so why not a kiss? I gripped his hair and pulled his head back, staring at his parted, wet lips. I'd needed his cock inside me, but his mouth, that I *wanted* with an aching desire almost as deep.

Jack's eyes opened and locked onto mine with a physical jolt I felt in every fibre of my body. I was going to kiss him. Then he moaned, "Fuck me. Ethan, please." He thrust his hips and hit my prostate.

"Jack," I gasped. "Yes." The bone deep craving to kiss him was still there, would always be there, but right now . . . this was nearly as good.

I rode him hard. Not fast, but deep and thoroughly, making sure every inch of him was inside me with every thrust. Every nerve in my body was alive and sparking. All the messy and wild emotions I'd felt in the kitchen flooded my veins and all I could do was hold Jack while they crashed through me. His arms kept me in one piece and his voice grounded me. I rode him and my own chaos until he groaned out, "Ethan!" and we came together.

CHAPTER TEN

I ended up belly down on the couch, Jack on his side, pressed into the back cushions so there was enough room I didn't tumble off. The blinds were pulled back on the balcony doors and I gazed at the sparkling lights of the city while Jack traced the scars on my back. We'd been quiet since our orgasms, moving in sync until we were comfortable together. It was just our breathing, the occasional creak of leather and the distant hum of Sydney at night. I had the tube of lube in my dangling hand, flipping it idly, end to end, the action soothing in its predictability.

"Ethan?"

The soft word roused me from a half-drowse. "Hmm?"

Jack's hand stroked down my spine. "Are you happy?"

I bumped my hips lazily under his touch. "Extremely."

A light smack. "I'm serious. Are you happy here? Living with me, doing this domestic thing."

Setting the lube down, I caught his hand and brought it around so I could hold it to my chest. "Extremely."

"Me too."

I kissed his knuckles. "You seem much happier with work lately."

"I don't know about happy. Resigned is probably more accurate." He sighed. "It's weird work. I'm a field asset. I find the information for the analysts to study. Or I act on what the analysts have worked out. I don't do the analysis. But that's all I'm doing now. Adam adds something to the profile and we spend two days going through all the evidence and statements looking for anything to do with it. Then he gets a different idea and it's back to the start."

"Sounds tedious."

"It is and it isn't. It's fascinating watching Adam pull all these disparate elements from different sources and create this image of a whole person he's never met." Jack's hand tightened around mine. "This killer, he's like none I've ever come across before. He's precise and methodical while breaking into the scene, but when he kills . . . It's manic. Anyone with the skills and knowledge to break and enter like that *knows* how to kill cleanly. The multiple stabbings isn't consistent with a killer who takes the time to move the victim to the shower first, so he can wash away evidence."

Jack continued to talk through the case but I stopped paying keen attention. Multiple stab wounds, use of the shower to remove evidence . . . it sounded familiar. It was only when I remembered Jack saying previously that the killer used Bible quotes that it all slotted into place.

While we lay there, I sent a message to Seven, demanding she respond, but got nothing back before Jack decided it was time to move things to the bedroom. He curled around me in bed and was quickly asleep. No longer able to even doze, I sent more messages to my silent sister, finally starting to worry.

Why would Two do a job in Seven's territory? I had, but that had been a tactical decision due to the psyche of the target. If the job was simply to execute targets under the guise of a serial killer, then I saw no reason why Seven wouldn't be able to perform the job.

At two a.m., Seven *ping*ed back.

"Are you all right?" I demanded silently, worming my way out of Jack's slack embrace and going to the living room.

"I'm not dead at least." There was no inflection in her words to hint at her mood.

"What did he do?" Neither of us needed to say his name.

After a pause, Seven sent, *"Broken arm, cracked ribs, bruised larynx."*

I sank down onto the couch where Jack and I had been so happy only a few hours ago. *"When did he hurt you?"*

"Two months ago. I'd just received the order for the two Sydney targets and was preparing when he found me."

Long enough she would be close to fully healed by now, thankfully, yet it meant there had been no recourse but to send someone else on the job. Two had likely volunteered to be the Judge even as he wiped Seven's blood off his hands.

"He's using the serial killer cover you set up in Melbourne," I told her.

"Naturally." This time there was a wry twist that made me chuckle, even through the growing darkness of realisation.

There was only one reason why Two had disabled Seven so he could come here. I had stopped him once from hurting Jack and Two did not like being told no.

"Be careful, One-three," Seven said seriously. *"He's even more unhinged than usual."*

"I know."

"Leave. Don't let him catch you."

"I can't." I wouldn't leave Jack unprotected while Two was after him. My only course was to convince Two to go home and forget both of us.

The silence stretched out so long I wondered if she had cut the connection, disgusted with my refusal to see reason, but then she sent, *"Good luck,"* and this time, I knew she was gone.

I sent a message to Nine, letting her know I'd contacted Seven and what Two was up to. Her response was rude and scathing but comforting all the same when she ended it with, *"Call when you need me to fish your ass out of hot water."*

Dejana called the next day and I dutifully returned to the sniper's nest. The best way of finding Two was to let him come to me and since he'd already found me twice while with Dejana, it seemed the quickest way. It took two sessions in the nest before he appeared.

"You're losing your touch," he said as he crawled up beside me, keeping out of sight of the client in the office across the street.

"I saw you on the street." I didn't shift my eye from the rifle site. If he'd wanted to sneak up on me he wouldn't have let me see him or hear him exit the stairwell.

"That's not what I meant."

"I know."

The current client finished her business and left. Dejana sat still, patiently waiting for the next one. She kept variable length windows between meetings and didn't tell me what they were, expecting me to be on constant watch. While we waited, Two rolled over and clasped his hands over his chest, looking up at the blue sky through his sunglasses, heaving great sighs every now and then. I ignored him.

"Is this what you really want to be doing, One-three?" he eventually asked.

Two wasn't talking about lying on a roof, covered by a tarp and pointing a rifle at various underworld targets. I didn't take the bait. The whole point of the exercise was to get Two out of the country, not let him inside my head.

"You're one of the best," he continued. "We were always better than the others. That's why I helped you when we were children. I knew you could be nearly as good as me, but only if you let me show you how."

The sole of my left foot itched. Two had tried his hardest to possess me back then. He had very nearly succeeded.

"I thought you were leaving once your job was done," I said as Dejana's next client entered the office.

"And I will."

What game was Two playing? Seven had said there were two targets and Jack talked about two victims of the Judge in Sydney. Did Two believe I wouldn't be able to find out he was lying?

"It's just that I worry about you, little brother. You never were . . . robust in matters of the heart. Remember what happened with Eleven? You didn't cope very well at all." His voice dropped to a pained whisper. "When I saw your back after the whipping . . . You could have died. Because of your foolishness, I nearly lost you. I don't want to go through that again."

I locked away every memory of Eleven and the months following his death and focused on the man sitting opposite Dejana. He wore a respectable suit and carried an attaché case, though he left it on the floor beside his chair. There was a small bulge in the top left of his jacket that could be an ill-concealed weapon, or a large billfold. Dejana showed no sign of concern.

Two rolled over and produced a pair of small binoculars. "You're going to have to kill this one."

He was right, and had it been Two with the rifle, the man would already be dead.

"Will you tell him tonight? When you go home to him and he asks about your day, will you say, 'I shot a man today'?"

My finger curled around the trigger of the rifle. The target hadn't made any suspicious moves but I could feel the coming action all the same. There was a sense of preparation to the angle of his torso, the spread of his legs. He was all but telescoping his reach for the weapon.

"Do you think if you eat enough of his butter chicken he'll finally let you kiss him?"

Bang!

I shot the client just as he went for his weapon. Dejana barely had a chance to signal before the window glass crazed into a million fractures and the bullet ploughed through and hit the bridge of the man's nose. He died instantly and I was up and moving before he'd even fallen out of the chair.

Two was after me a hair's breadth later, a knife in one hand, expression blank. I parried his thrusts with the rifle, giving myself room to break away. Dropping the cumbersome weapon, I drew an Eagle.

My brother froze, but a smile curled his full lips up. "You won't shoot me."

I settled into a shooter's stance, gun hand supported in the other. As I had with the target, I aimed for the bridge of Two's nose. It was instant death.

"You won't shoot me," he repeated, firmer. "You don't have the guts to even try."

Then he came at me.

Unlike the previous fight, this one was brutal. It felt as if Two was really trying to kill me. Which was something I'd rarely feared from him. I'd learned very quickly that Two's only understanding of how to deal with his emotions was through pain. I disagreed with him, so he hurt me until I stopped.

My sisters were right. I should never have let Two get this close. This fight had to stop before it got any worse.

I knocked aside a vicious thrust from the knife with my forearm, earning a slice in the material of my suit jacket for my troubles.

It didn't reach skin but Two's other fist connected with my ribs. I barely deflected the next slash from his weapon and Two pressed the advantage, driving me backwards. Before I knew it, my back was to the wall of the plant room. The point of Two's knife landed in the hollow at the base of my throat.

Everything went still, our gazes locked through the dark lenses of our sunglasses. All it would take was a single thrust and I would be dead. I lowered my head.

After several long heartbeats, the pressure of the sharp blade tip lessened, then Two stood back and sheathed the knife.

"You will come home with me," he said. "You've played with the spy for long enough. It's time you returned to what you were born to be."

"I'm not going anywhere with you."

Two laughed, short and bitter. "Remember the last time you said that to me? Remember what happened not even two weeks later?"

I shook my head, still not meeting his gaze. "I mean it this time. I've quit. I'm staying here with Jack, forever."

"Why?" He sounded honestly perplexed.

"Because he's the only one who's ever made me happy."

The words were barely out of my mouth before Two slammed up against me again. Forearm across my throat, the point of his knife pressing into my ribs, Two breathing hard, lips peeled back from clenched teeth. His knife hand trembled, as if he had to restrain it forcefully.

"He doesn't love you, One-three. He can make you all the curries you want, but he hasn't taken you to his special place." Two sneered at my startled gasp. "You don't know about it, do you? The place he goes to think and *cry*. You have nothing to stay for. You will come home, even if you have to crawl to do it. I'll make sure of it."

"I won't do it."

"Oh, you will. You'll have no choice."

"What do you mean?"

Two backed off slowly, letting the tip of the blade drag down my torso, tearing a ragged line in the cotton of my jacket. "You're not the only one who can set a trap, little brother." He smiled, turned and left the roof top.

As the door closed behind him, a message *ping*ed into my implant. Knowing it was from Two, I opened it, bracing for whatever he wanted to torture me with.

It was a single image of two men at a table in a pub. Surrounded by the golden light of low wattage bulbs, they looked intimate as the blond leaned in close, and the other man laughed, his Indian features lit up with genuine amusement.

CHAPTER ELEVEN

Dejana's clean-up crew took care of the client's body, as they had that of the shooter at the park. She thanked me for my fast action by releasing another lump sum of money and hinting she wouldn't require my services for several days at least. This attacker had gotten too close and she needed to find an uncompromised location for her meetings—and root out the source of the threat.

All of which was perfectly fine with me. I had more important matters to deal with now.

I made it back to the garage without picking up a police tail, so I tucked Victoria away out of sight and took the Monaro out. She had been ready to go for a couple of days and only required a set of new tyres before she was perfect, but right then, I needed a car not easily connected to me.

Driving past the Surry Hills LAC, I found Jack's Ninja. I kept an eye on it for the rest of the afternoon, making sure he didn't leave early.

The pieces had finally fallen into place. Why Two had ensured he took the job in Sydney and why he was still here even though two victims were dead. One of those victims hadn't been a sanctioned Cabal target. It was so obvious now. The army captain had been killed simply to draw Jack into the search for the Judge—the search for Two.

Two had set a trap, and Jack was his target.

Jack emerged late in the day, accompanied by the other man from Two's image. Blond, handsome, not quite as tall as Jack. Unwilling to show the first picture to anyone else, I snapped an image of him with my implant and sent it to Seven with a request for ID. It had to be Adam Quinn, but I needed to be certain.

The two of them got onto the Ninja with practiced ease. My heart clenched at the sight. I'd hadn't ridden with Jack on his bike and yet this man, this stranger, was very comfortable wrapping his arms around Jack's waist and leaning on him. My fingers inched towards the Eagle under my left arm.

Jack turned the bike into the traffic and quickly wove his way through the cars. It was a challenge keeping up, but it let me know I was his only tail.

They stopped at a pub and went in together. Parking further up the street, I followed them in. As with tailing them, keeping out of Jack's sight in the close interior of the pub was difficult. He didn't note me, however. Not even when Seven sent confirmation that the blond man was Dr. Adam Quinn and I was sure I stared daggers at him for a full five minutes. Thankfully, all they did was talk and drink, though Jack imbibed substantially less than the other man.

Unable to watch more of them chatting and laughing freely, I left. After exchanging the Monaro for Victoria, I went back to Leichhardt. Stripping out of my wrecked suit revealed the blooming bruises of Two's attack. Wearing pyjama bottoms and a T-shirt, I got into bed and pretended to be asleep when Jack finally came in. He undressed quietly and made a few tentative advances before accepting my sleepy brush off and settling for curling up against my back.

I wanted to roll over and hold him, tell him how I felt and ask him if he felt the same way. I wanted to ask him if he had feelings for Quinn. All I did was wait until he was deeply asleep, slid out of bed and spent the night checking the security system.

There were no signs of anyone breaching it, except for a single foreign camera on the balcony, facing inwards, which explained how Two knew about our dinner and how I'd almost kissed Jack.

I felt sick knowing Two had seen everything that night, but worse, the fact that he'd circumvented my external security to place even one camera was simply terrifying.

Short of iron grates on the door and windows and sentry guns, there was very little else I could do to Jack's apartment to make it more secure. It hadn't been designed with maximum safety in mind.

Unlike the Bathurst Street penthouse. I had to finish making it liveable, in between keeping Jack out of Two's trap and doing my best to divert Two's attention away from his goal. I would let him find me

every couple of days and encourage him to finish the job and leave—
anyway I could.

"You can't keep it up for long," Nine said when she got in touch a
week into the new arrangement. *"It'll just take one time for him to not
hold back and . . ."* She made a screechy noise I assumed was a knife
across my throat.

I rolled more paint onto the wall in the penthouse main bedroom,
covering up the new plaster over the extra wires I'd installed. My back
twinged where Two had landed a particularly powerful kick. "He
doesn't want to kill me." Although it felt like it at times. Ignoring
the pain, I finished concealing the work site. This was the final bit of
touch-up required, and then I would have the furnishings delivered.
A couple more days and Jack and I would be able to move in.

"Who knows what that the freak wants," she muttered, then louder,
*"He doesn't have to kill you, just chop off something important. Don't be
an idiot, One-three. Two's not going to leave you alone. You've got to get
away. Go somewhere he won't find you."*

"I'm not leaving. This is where I want to be and my decision has
nothing to do with him."

*"You're crazy, but not delusional. You know he's not reasonable, ever,
and even less so where you're concerned. He thinks you're his to do with as
he pleases, remember."*

A phantom pain ran through my left foot. Followed by real pain
as I stood and bumped a bruise on the cupboard door. "I'm doing my
best to let him know how wrong he is."

Nine sighed. *"No, you're not. You're just giving him what he wants.
Your time. Your focus. Your thoughts. Getting away from him is your only
option."*

"I won't leave Jack." Even if I wondered if he was leaving me.
He had been spending more and more time with Quinn outside of
work, time in which I tortured myself by watching them. Jack didn't
frown or argue with him, as he did with me lately. He didn't laugh at
much I said anymore. Even his attempts to initiate sex had dwindled
until now he just sighed and kissed whatever body part of mine was

easiest before falling asleep beside me. "Especially not while Two's after him."

"*Then take him with you.*"

"He doesn't deserve a life on the run."

There was a long silence from Nine's end of the connection. I gave her all the time she needed, knowing where her mind had gone. I wasn't the only one who'd found someone outside of our strange and dangerous family to care about.

"*Shouldn't that be his decision?*" she eventually asked, tone bitter as she used my slightly paraphrased words against me.

"I already know his answer. I asked him once if he would scramble with me and he said he wouldn't."

Though I wanted to believe that answer had changed. So much had happened between us since then. So many good things that were surely enough to counteract the current difficulties. I knew I was hurting Jack with my behaviour but it was the only way I knew to keep him safe, even if it was also pushing him away and towards another man. I just had to hope our history outweighed whatever connection Jack may have formed with the profiler over the past month.

Nine growled something inarticulate, then snapped, "*Fine. I'll be there in a couple of days. Don't let Two kill you before then.*"

"You don't have to come here, Nine. I can take care of this."

"*Clearly, you can't. He's already hurt Seven, and you're letting him close with you. You need me to sort this out.*"

I made a few more protests but Nine was stubborn when she decided to do something and, in truth, I wanted her here. Another set of eyes on Jack could only be a good thing. And if anyone was ever going to get an advantage over Two, it was Nine.

Whether it was knowing Nine was on her way or worry that Jack was really pulling away from me, I turned into his hesitant touch that night. He was sweet and gentle as he removed my clothes, brushing fingertips and lips over the fading bruises as he moved downwards and sucked my cock into his warm mouth. In those minutes everything was perfect. Between us, in that room, with the world. I didn't care about

Quinn or Two. All that mattered was Jack and the way he showed me how much he still wanted me, still cared about my pleasure, still needed me when he sank into my body with a drawn out, husky, "Ethan," and held me tight until we came together.

Afterwards was another matter, however.

"Don't give me any bullshit this time." Jack traced one of the fresher bruises on my lower ribs. "You aren't clumsy, you can't spend *that* much time under Victoria's bonnet and you sure as shit don't bruise easily. What the fuck is going on?"

I wanted to tell him the truth, but I knew how he would react. He'd want to go out and hunt down Two—more directly than he was now, albeit unknowingly—and that wouldn't work well for him. Jack was the finest soldier I'd ever met and very nearly a match for me in combat. He wouldn't prevail against Two.

"Jesus, Ethan." Jack pressed his forehead into my belly while he drew in several deep, calming breaths. "I'm worried, that's all. I need you to be okay. Otherwise, I don't—" He cut himself off and kissed my skin, hard and lingering.

I ran my hand through his hair and nearly told him I loved him, but what came out was, "It's nothing to be worried about, Jack. I'm just . . . it's a surprise. For you."

He kissed a still livid bruise on my left flank. "What sort of surprise entails this?"

"A good one, I hope." The penthouse was almost ready and when I took him there, I would tell him I loved him. I would show him how much I trusted him.

Jack moved up and caught my gaze. His dark eyes swam with concern. "Nothing is worth you getting hurt."

How could I ever doubt how he felt about me when I saw those beautiful eyes? "Some things are worth it."

"Like what?"

For what felt like the first time in an eternity, I said honestly, "Like you, Jack."

Which resulted in Jack holding me so tight through the night I couldn't get out of bed to check the apartment. Instead I had to lie there and listen to his breathing and when a dream shook his limbs, hold him and whisper that I was there and not going anywhere.

The conversation didn't appease Jack's worries, however. Especially not when Two managed to nick me with his knife a day later and Jack refused to accept I'd cut my neck shaving. Added to that stress, Nine was delayed. Her way into Australia was apparently blocked by a rather pesky navy frigate doing manoeuvres off the West Australian coast. She assured me she would find a way around them but I wondered if she would get here quick enough as I watched Jack and Quinn get drunk together one night.

I sat in a shadowed corner of the usual pub as Quinn poured more and more alcohol down Jack's throat and got closer and closer. Their heads were bowed towards each other and although I had no hope of hearing the conversation or reading their lips, I knew it had to be very intense. Despite his inebriation, Jack listened intently to whatever the profiler was saying, asking questions and nodding often.

When they stood, I let them leave first, then followed, just in time to hear Quinn drunkenly proclaim, "He's okay, I guess. 'Snot you, though. Come on, don'tcha wanna fuck my mouth again?"

My heart plummeted and all my training fled. I could not ignore that implication and keep within the parameters of the job. Not this time. This wasn't Two needling me, or a leg cramp, or any one of a hundred other possible distractions. Nothing I'd learned from the Cabal could help me here.

I left Jack vulnerable to Two—and Quinn—and just walked.

Naturally, Two found me.

"He didn't tell you, did he," he said softly as he fell into step beside me.

I didn't even have the wherewithal to react to his mere presence, let alone the words. All I knew was at least he wasn't near Jack while he was compromised.

"It was quite the affair I believe. The good doctor has been pining ever since." Two cocked his head quizzically. "Isn't it interesting that they're working together on the same case?"

The trap Two had dug for Jack was deep indeed.

"Why are you doing this?" I asked.

"Because you need to remember where you belong. It isn't here, with him. Someone who cheats on you, who uses you just for sex." Two lowered his voice even further. "I mean, there has to be a reason why he won't let you kiss him."

One of the Eagles was in my hand without thought. I spun and pressed my shoulder into Two's chest, the barrel of the gun shoved into his belly. Two froze. Anyone passing us on the street probably believed we were a couple, about to kiss.

"You will finish your job and you will not do it as the Judge. Don't give them any reason to connect it to their case. Do that and leave Sydney. And then leave Australia at the first opportunity and never return," I hissed. "Or I will kill you."

Two's chuckle sounded forced. "You can't. You've already proven that, or have you forgotten the final test?"

I clicked off the safety.

"All right!" Hands raised, Two back off and I had to put the gun away swiftly or risk inciting a general panic. "I see you're serious."

"Deadly."

Two's smile was wide as he walked backwards several more paces. "Anything for you, little brother." Then he turned and continued away. I watched him go until he was out of sight.

Even taking a meandering course back to the Monaro to lose any tails, and then another on the way to Leichhardt, I beat Jack back to the apartment. Now that I knew the full extent Two had gone to in order to build this trap, I understood Jack wasn't in immediate physical danger. Not while Two was amused with the game he'd set up.

The situation wouldn't stay that way forever, though. Two had come to make sure I left with him, and the best way to do that was to force Jack into betraying me. None of this was Jack's fault. But knowing that didn't make watching Jack stagger home any less painful. At least he was here and not wherever the profiler was.

We had to talk. It was time for truths on both sides.

"Jack, you're late."

Jack wove a slight zig zag to the fridge and got a bottle of water. "I never said what time I'd be home." His attempt at enunciation was excruciating.

"I hope you didn't ride home in this state." Saving him from Two would be for nothing if he killed himself on that old bike.

"Got a taxi." He surrendered his attempt at opening the bottle and settled on a comical leer. "Missed you, baby. Let's fuck."

The following conversation went about as well as it could. Nevertheless I took pity on him and steered him into the bedroom. Jack tried to cajole me into sex but gave up when I checked him for a fever.

"I'm fine. I'm just drunk."

At last, some honesty. I wondered how far it would reach. "You went drinking with Adam, I suppose."

Jack rolled away from me. "He's part of my job. Gotta pretend to be his friend."

What I'd witnessed in that pub over the past weeks wasn't Jack acting. He genuinely liked the other man. Enough, apparently, to sleep with him at some previous point. I was all but convinced it wasn't happening now. All but . . .

"That's all right, Jack. I understand." I did, even if I wasn't comfortable with it. "I was, however, hoping you could spend tomorrow with me."

"Can't. Working. You know that."

"Could you take a day off? Don't you Aussies pride yourself on taking 'sickies'?"

"I'm on an important case," Jack moaned. "I can't just pretend to be sick for you."

Jack hadn't put this sort of wall between us in a long time. It hurt more than one of Two's blows. More than all of them together. Was he doing this because of Quinn? Or had I forced him to do this with my paranoid behaviour and mysterious bruises? Because he wondered if I was an unhinged killer? Either way, I needed to try again. We had to talk, and it had to be somewhere away from our known routines so Two had less of a chance of following us.

"I've booked track time at Wakefield tomorrow." I hadn't, but I knew the track manager well enough he'd fit me in. "It takes a couple of hours to get there, so going is a whole-day endeavour. I'd very much appreciate it if you would come with me." I touched his shoulder gently. "I need to drive, Jack, and I think I need you there with me." Which was true. I hadn't unleashed Victoria—or myself—in a long time. I needed to feel in control of *something* and on the racetrack was where that happened the most.

Jack's shoulder tensed under my hand. "I'd like to go with you. I can't, though. Things are at a vital stage of the case." He clumsily grabbed my hand and kissed it. "You go. Do a lap for me, too, okay."

Yes, the walls from our early relationship were being built again. The walls he'd had when he slept with other men.

Retrieving my hand, I stood. "As you wish, Jack."

He'd passed out before I'd even reached the bedroom door—before he'd realised I wasn't getting into bed with him.

CHAPTER TWELVE

I spent the night watching over Jack from a distance, fairly certain Two didn't mean him physical harm—yet. At dawn, I left Sydney and headed for Wakefield, hoping to find some measure of peace in the drive. Sadly the limits on the speed didn't help me and I needed the race track. I missed the autobahn.

In the midst of negotiating my last-minute request for track time, Jack called.

"Jack," I answered silently as Phil, the manager, checked the schedule for me. It didn't even enter my mind to ignore the call. I was upset and confused, but not about to let Jack think I wasn't able to respond.

That sentiment, however, didn't make it into my tone and Jack's response was an almost panicked, *"I'm sorry."*

I could imagine how he felt, waking up to find me gone, especially if he had any memory of his actions the previous night. Worried, yes. Ashamed, hopefully. Before I could reply Phil offered me an opening in fifteen minutes and another later in the afternoon. As I signed up for both, Jack rushed on with his apology.

"I was a total dickhead last night. No excuses. Except for, well, I told you I would fuck something up sooner or later. I'd really like to make it up to you. Can you come home?"

"I'm afraid not, Jack. I'm not in Sydney."

"Fuck." Jack sounded like he was on the verge of tears. *"I'm really sorry. I don't want you to leave."*

Oh. *"I'm still in the country, Jack, at Wakefield. My track time starts in fifteen minutes. I will be back this evening."*

"Jesus. Don't scare me like that."

He was so desperately relieved I almost smiled. *"Oh, I think you have a few more scares coming."*

"Yeah, I reckon I do. I'm glad you are getting to race."

"Yes, well. The booking fee is non-refundable."

"I'm going to take the day off, like you wanted me to. I could meet you down there."

My heart leaped at the thought of Jack here. I would race and have Jack and feel complete and content. But that small concern from the start of this enterprise reared back up. What if I couldn't do this alone? What if it was only Jack propping me up? Once, racing my cars was all I needed to centre myself. I needed to know that was still true.

"I don't think so, Jack. Right now, I'd rather be alone."

"Okay. Anything else I can do to show you how sorry I am? Do you want butter chicken for dinner?"

"I'm not sure. I will let you know."

"I'll see you tonight, then?"

I sighed. *"Yes, you will."*

"Drive safely."

He was trying so hard. *"Where's the fun in that?"*

It took barely four laps for the speed, and the control it required, to work its usual magic. I felt steady for the first time in weeks, even as Victoria's vibrations spread through me. She ran well, except for a slight hitch when shifting into sixth. I spent several laps monitoring it, letting the puzzle consume my mind.

When I pulled into pit lane and coasted into the space assigned to me, I had a good idea of what was happening in the engine. Ten minutes under the bonnet confirmed my thoughts and I spent a couple of hours immersed in fixing the issue. When it was done, I still had an hour or so before my next track time, so I sat in the stands and watched a parade of cars go round and round. Even judging other drivers wasn't enough to keep my thoughts centred wholly on the track.

Jack liked the profiler. I had gathered more than enough evidence over the past weeks to confirm it. From how Jack talked about him to the way he smiled at the man when they sat in the pub together. I fixated on how close the other man got when he rode on the back of Jack's bike, and the way Jack didn't stop him. It was friendship, yes, but it could also be so much more than that.

It wasn't hard to see that Jack was happy when he was with him. Just as it was obvious he had never thought "serial killer" when talking to him. The profiler didn't come with dangerous baggage in the form a deranged brother and the global-wide secret organisation that created him. He likely didn't need to hurl a high-powered vehicle around a racetrack at ludicrous speeds just to feel in control of something. He would let Jack touch him in public, he wouldn't spend nights obsessed with the lack of locks on the door or fixate on the fact the same car had parked outside three days in a row. He wouldn't be so scared about this new and amazing part of his life it sent him right back to the job he'd tried to leave over and over in the past.

When it was my turn on the track again, I slammed Victoria through a dozen rough and hard circuits, straining the fixes I'd made. She handled it beautifully, coming out the other side as perfect as she'd gone in.

This I could do and did it very well. I had my cars, I had Nine's bike I could take apart and put back together blindfolded. I'd go back to Austria and just be a mechanic, happy and safe. Jack would be very happy with the profiler and much safer without me here endangering him with my mere presence. I wouldn't have to worry about Dejana keeping her promise to excise me from the Cabal once and for all. I wouldn't have to worry about Jack thinking I was no better than a murderer.

I let the realisation wash through me, let it resonate with the roar of Victoria's engine and the shiver in her body as she glided around corners and showed off her raw power on the straights.

Jack should be happy. He deserved it after all he'd been through. If I let Jack go, he would finally have that and I could go back to the life I knew, where I wasn't constantly second guessing myself or confused or lost. The world where I would never know another kind touch, or surging passion, or the tranquillity of hearing Jack breathe beside me at night.

But he'd be better off, and I wouldn't have to worry about him, or myself, any more.

Jack was waiting for me in the garage when I got to the apartment building, though he appeared to have been working out. Sweat made the thin material of his T-shirt cling to the dips and curves of his muscular torso and I sat boneless in the car, staring at his body as he approached. The sight made all of my convictions crumble.

It wasn't just the beautiful body, or the contrite expression, or the vaguely hopeful smile he gave me as I got out of the car. It was simply that he was here, clearly waiting for me, hoping I would return.

He was here, not at work, and not with Quinn. Here for me.

My original goal in going to Wakefield had been to give us a place to talk away from potential eavesdroppers. I had let myself forget that, let my fears override everything else. Yes, Jack deserved to be happy, but so did I. Could Jack and I be happy together?

Only if I found out the truth first. We needed to talk. To be honest with each other.

"Jack." I faced him, car between us.

"Ethan. I'm sorry."

"I know you are."

Jack winced and looked away. After an awkward moment he asked about Victoria, which helped break the brittle atmosphere a tad. Before it could get worse, though, I suggested we go upstairs to talk privately. We fell into familiar and trusted patterns on the way to the apartment and by the time we were behind a locked and secured door, Jack had lost some of his tension. His shoulders slumped as he drifted around the kitchen counter and leaned on it, appearing to need the solid support. He looked so defeated in that moment, I knew I had to go first. I had to explain and hope he understood.

It still took a few moments to gather the words and I couldn't look at Jack while I did so. His big brown eyes were working too hard to undo all my best intentions. Even without seeing him, I felt him in every bone of my body, in the way my blood seemed to pull towards him. It was hard to resist the desire to just go to him and beg for him to touch me. The physical connection between us had always been easy. Too easy at times, but I was learning that wasn't enough.

"I want to be here. I came with the expectation that this was it for me. We'd be together and nothing else would matter. I should have known better. There are things that can't be escaped, and the past is one of them." Particularly the men in both our histories. "I'm trying. I really am, but I don't know what I'm doing. You know your place in the world. You have your work, which you believe in, and a family you want to protect, no matter how distant they are. You have friends that care about you. Right now, all I have is you."

Jack made a soft noise, perhaps in sympathy, or protest, I wasn't sure. All I knew for certain was how much it hurt to admit this, how much it hurt to do this to Jack again. If I was going to get the truth out of him, though, I had to do it.

"I thought I could do this. Be what you wanted. Needed. But clearly, I'm failing." In so many ways, so it was time to go back to something else I knew how to do well.

"Ethan," Jack said, tone ragged with pain.

"Are you sleeping with Adam Quinn?"

As intended, the sudden question threw him. Jack floundered and his incredulous "What?" was full of honest surprise.

With the blinds drawn on the balcony doors it was dim enough I didn't need my glasses, and I needed to see Jack clearly, to see his reactions. He was right where I needed him, off balance, so I pressed the point.

"You talk about him all the time. He's part of your current job, yes, but you spend a lot of time with him outside of the demands of the strike force."

"Yeah, but it's still part of the job. Being friendly—"

"You don't have dinner with Senior Sergeant Stephanie Phelps, but she's part of the job."

"No, but—"

"And unless you're hiding something big, I don't believe you ever slept with her before."

Jack blinked at me. "What the fuck are you talking about?"

I settled into the role just as I'd settled into Victoria's driver's seat and pushed her to wild speeds. "I know you've slept with him before."

And just like that night we first met, Jack responded by slipping into his SAS lieutenant role.

"Okay," he said patiently. "Yeah, I fucked him a couple of times, way back before you and I got serious. You knew I saw other men sometimes back then. How did you know about Adam, though? Were you spying on me?"

"You don't want me to answer that."

Jack shook his head angrily. "Actually, I think I do."

He was right. I had wanted to think I was protecting Jack, but I had been spying. "You haven't answered my question. Are you sleeping with him now?"

A world of thoughts flashed through Jack's eyes as he watched me. Whatever they were, they made his hands clench on the counter and his shoulders stiffen. Then, just as suddenly, the tension melted away from him and he said, simply and honestly, "No."

He saw through my plan. As he'd always done. No matter the shields I put up or the walls I hid behind, Jack saw *me*. All the scars and the weapons and the fake names meant nothing to him. Even after I'd hurt him.

How could I ever think to leave that sort of connection?

Jack came around the counter and stood in front of me, close but not touching. "I'm not sleeping with him, or anyone else. I don't want to. I want this, too. Us. So much it scares me sometimes."

And there it was. Fear. The truth behind so much. I'd let my fears consume me at the racetrack, and never once considered Jack might be feeling the same way.

"Me too," I admitted. "I never used to get scared, Jack. Not for a very long time, at least. Then I met you, and suddenly there was so much I didn't know, *couldn't* know, and that . . . frightened me. I didn't know if whenever I went to you I would be welcomed or not, or perhaps find you already with someone else."

I was so grateful that had never happened but wondering just how Two knew of Jack and the profiler sent a shudder through me.

"I didn't know, still don't, if you would get tired of my . . . oddities and want nothing more to do with me. Each time you let me into your home, into your life, I didn't know why you would do that for me. And *he* is so much better for you. He's not a liability to you. He's not here on a fake passport. He's not messed up."

Jack swore quietly and it sounded like agreement.

"That's what I did today, Jack. I drove and it helped me decide that if you were with him, I'd walk away. You'd be safer. And happy. And I could stop being so scared." I pulled in a ragged breath and so did Jack. "But when I got out of the car and saw you waiting for me, I changed my mind. In spite of the pain and the risk, in spite of everything and every*one* else, I want this. I don't know what I'm doing, Jack, but I want to keep trying. With you."

We reached for each other at the same time and ended up on the floor, tangled in a mess that seemed to perfectly capture our whole relationship.

"Well, I don't know about anyone else, but I think we're certainly a danger to ourselves."

Jack's words so closely mirrored my thoughts it surprised a laugh out of me. With a few minor adjustments, we lay somewhat more comfortably and just held each other.

"Hey, are we good?"

Jack's fingers in my hair derailed my cognitive functions for a moment. When I could, I said, "Yes, we're good."

"Great. Can we get up, then? I'm lying on something that's digging into my arse."

It turned out to be a small shifter that had fallen out of my pocket, which Jack teased me about and then laughed at my attempt to turn it into a seduction.

Right then, I knew I'd made the right decision. How could I have ever thought I would be able to live without this? Jack may have been happier—or at least safer—with Quinn, but surely moments like this were worth the occasional pain.

"McIntosh called me in today," Jack said when he'd finished making me blush. "They've decided working with the strike force isn't worth our time anymore. The Office is no longer interested in the Judge or Infinity."

Blast. Two liked being ignored as much as he liked being disagreed with. Hopefully this wouldn't hinder his compliance with my demands.

"Ethan? Isn't that good news?"

"Of course it is." It was, because it would mean Jack wasn't directly entangled in Two's plot anymore.

"How about if I sweeten it with a bonus of me having a week off work?"

I smiled. If I could keep Jack out of sight for a week, Two would have absolutely no recourse but to give up his game. The Cabal wouldn't stand for his delaying in finishing the job much longer. This was perfect. And I was fairly certain I knew how to keep Jack from wanting to leave the apartment.

Standing, I pulled off my shirt and headed for the bedroom. "That is incredibly good news. Let's celebrate."

CHAPTER THIRTEEN

How had it gone so wrong so quickly? Three short but intensely good days of pure bliss and now... *this*.

It was my fault. Jack had been pressed against me, between my legs as I sat on the kitchen counter, so out of my mind with the firm belief he was about to kiss me I hadn't cared about the open door. I'd left us vulnerable right as a threat appeared. Quinn. The man I'd almost lost Jack to, reappearing just when everything had been so perfect.

Instinct had driven me. Throw Jack off, find weapons, eliminate the threat. Jack had stopped me though. He'd put himself between the profiler and my guns. He'd tackled me to the floor rather than let me attack.

So here I was, gripping the edge of the bathroom sink, needing the solidity to tether me, while Jack dealt with the threat. The need to move, to eliminate the danger, still fired through my body like a physical force. The curve of the counter edge nestled into the space between thumb and forefinger like the butt of a gun. Like the grip of the gun I'd pointed at Adam Quinn.

"It's not his fault," the image in the mirror told me but I shook my head, unable to fully believe it right then. He was a threat to everything I loved and I only knew one way to deal with it.

Hunt and kill.

It would be easy to do. The target was predictable and careless. Reckless too, the way he'd just stood in the doorway while two weapons were trained on him. Stubborn, as well, because he'd persisted in arguing while Jack told him to leave. All easy traits to exploit. All traits that would make it so easy to stalk him, set my sight, and pull the trigger. So easy.

Calm settled over me. My hold on the counter eased and my spine straightened. The beat of my heart slowed, and my breaths deepened.

This I could do and do well. I wouldn't mess this up as I had everything else.

A high-pitched whine cut through the silence, followed by a scrabble of little claws at the base of the bathroom door.

Shorty. Here because Rocco Cesare trusted us to look after his beloved companion while he was away. Because he thought I was a good enough man to call "son."

All of the conviction to kill rushed out of me. I sank into a crouch, head bowed, hands in my hair, fingers digging into my scalp.

This wasn't me. Not anymore. The blind reliance on skills and thoughts drummed into me as a child hadn't held sway in a long time. Not since Eleven, and the whipping, and Moraitis. It'd had even less control of me since meeting Jack. I had been yearning for a way out of the life created for me by the Cabal ever since I'd understood just what they were doing. It hadn't been until Jack looked at Ethan Blade and saw not just a remorseless killer for hire but a man, that I'd known I could truly do it.

And yet here I was. Reduced to the instinctual killer in one stupid moment, ready to go after an innocent person and end them. Because I'd been careless. Because I'd been so caught up in Jack and our cosy, warm world within the apartment I'd failed to see the weakness in the perimeter. If the target—if *Quinn* could find Jack's place, if he could walk right up to the front door and look in at us, then anyone could. It clearly hadn't taken anyone of Two's standards to find us and get into a position to pose a serious threat.

I couldn't do this. Couldn't be here with Jack. Not now, with Quinn and Two in the city.

Shorty gave a surprised bark when I opened the door, then immediately scrabbled at my leg, whining. I picked him up and he wiggled frantically until he could lick my chin and snuffle at my neck, looking to comfort as well as needing it return. I tucked the squirming body under one arm and carefully scouted the apartment.

Quinn was gone, as was Jack. There was no doubt that Jack had gone after the man to rage at him. He always did find the most inappropriate outlet for his anger.

Assured the place was free of threats, I set Shorty down, but he kept close by as I packed up my gear. The dachshund knew what was going on and he kept staring at me with his big dark eyes, pleading with me to stay. He even climbed into one of the bags and curled up tight. I left him there until the very last moment, until I'd put everything back where it had been before I moved in. Shorty grumbled about being removed, bounced excitedly when I pulled out his leash, then whined pitifully when I tied it to the knob of the downstairs neighbour whom I knew occasionally looked after him while Rocco was away.

Then I left. Again. I wouldn't be back for a long time.

I'd nearly killed an innocent person. Like a serial killer.

I was well ensconced behind the security of the Bathurst Street penthouse when Jack's call *ping*ed my implant.

"Jack." I schooled myself to simply not beg him to come to me, to tell me he still wanted me. The penthouse wasn't finished yet and after all the ways I'd failed him already, I wanted to give him something perfect for once.

"Are you okay?"

"I'm fine."

"I yelled at Adam for a while."

That made me smile slightly. "I imagine you did."

"He won't be back. Will you?"

Much as Shorty had, I curled up tighter on the huge bed until the urge to weep passed. "I don't know. I can't feel safe there, Jack. I'm sorry."

"Don't be." His tone was warm and understanding. *"I know you can't. Are you safe now?"*

I didn't deserve him. "I am."

"Good. Can I come to you?"

It was hard, but at the same time, easy. I wanted him so badly it hurt, but right then, having him near would also hurt because he would so easily forgive me for what I'd done.

"Not yet," I managed. "I need to be on my own for a while. I left Shorty with Mrs. Langridge on the first floor. Please fetch him back. You shouldn't be alone because of me."

"Okay." His steady tone wavered a bit. *"Just . . . let me know how you're doing."*

"I will. See you soon, Jack." It was the truth. I was going to get myself sorted out, then I would bring Jack here and show him in no uncertain way how I felt about him.

I lost myself in putting the finishing touches on the penthouse. The furnishings had all arrived and I spent a couple of days arranging and rearranging everything until the flow felt right. There were clear paths to the various weapons caches, which I ran through until the moves were second nature. I tested the security systems daily, plotted out escape routes and ensured I could enter and leave the penthouse and building without being seen.

Jack and I talked every day. Sometimes only for minutes, other times for hours. He tried to initiate phone sex a couple of times, but it was always derailed by my laughter. It felt so ridiculous, especially when he was a mere twenty-minute drive away. I lost count of the amount of times I nearly begged him to come here, but each time it was easy to resist. I trusted my instincts on this at least. We were talking and I was getting myself under control again. The knowledge that Jack was working with Quinn again didn't even bother me. Well, it did, but not as much.

On day six I ventured out of the penthouse and went to the garage. Ken trundled down to meet me.

"Was wondering if you'd be back." He eyed Victoria like she was a swan amongst the ducks. In this establishment, she was.

"I'm paid up to the end of the month."

"Yeah, but I wondered if you'd finally been picked up by the cops or something."

"Has that policeman been back?"

"Nah, but I just thought that meant they'd got you."

Across the way, a garage door opened and a woman wheeled a black Ducati out. I wasn't as familiar with bike models as I was cars, but I knew this was a Panigale, a cousin of Nine's SuperSport S.

Leaving Ken mumbling to himself about how he couldn't have the cops just showing up any old time, I went to get a closer look at the bike.

"It's for sale, if you're interested," the woman said in a smoke-roughened voice.

I crouched and checked out the body of the machine. "I might be. Why are you selling it?" I almost didn't care. The image of Jack astride the bike had taken hold and wouldn't let me go. He loved his Ninja, had held onto it longer than he probably should have, but this was elegant and sleek and I knew more about Ducatis than I did Kawasakis. I would love to maintain his bike for him.

"Can't afford it," she muttered. "My son bought it when he had a job, and now he doesn't, so it's gotta go."

Within minutes, I was on the bike and taking it for a test ride. It hadn't been well cared for, clearly, but the potential was still there within the two cylinders and the gear and chain drive system. I loved my cars above all other vehicles, but there was a wildness to racing a motorbike that you didn't get with a car. The inherent danger of being so exposed to the hard world flying by in a blur was a deep thrill but it was an exercise in closer control as well. Riding required a different sort of focus to racing a car that had never suited my needs as well.

Coasting back into the complex, I decided to buy the bike. It wouldn't take much work to get it back up to showroom quality and I would love to see Jack's face when I gave it to him. His birthday was two weeks away, giving me plenty of time.

Ken had disappeared again, thankfully, and I organised the sale with the woman quickly. I spent a wonderful afternoon going over the Ducati and making a list of the parts and equipment needed. I bought everything I would need on the way back to the penthouse, showered and then went to find Jack.

It happened without any worry or second-guessing. Just a natural desire to see the person I'd been thinking about all day, a shivering anticipation of simply being near him again. He was, of course, at Quinn's hotel, discreetly working on the Judge case again. I circled the block twice and the third time found a park directly in front of the building. I'd no sooner pulled in when Jack exited the hotel, scowling irritably. The expression morphed into a wide smile when he saw Victoria, however, and into an even wider grin when I opened the door and told him to hurry up.

Jack got in faster than I'd ever seen him move before. "Hey."

He had yet to lose or lessen his smile. How had I managed to stay away from him for a week? "Close the door, Jack. We have somewhere to be."

Once we were underway, Jack settled a hand on my thigh and asked, "Where are we going?"

"It's a surprise." I covered his hand with mine, thinking about how he would react to the penthouse, and to the other thing I wanted to surprise him with.

Jack grumbled a bit, but it was half-hearted and purely for form because he kissed my knuckles and then said he had a surprise for me as well. Thankfully I didn't have to wait long as we'd arrived at Bathurst Street. I showed Jack the private lift and once inside, alone and secure, he held me.

All the worry and fear from the past week faded into a small, ignorable mote in the back of my head the moment Jack pressed his face into my neck. I grabbed onto him, my hands locking into his shirt like he was a lifeline.

"I missed you," I whispered. "So much."

Jack kissed my neck. "You did?"

He was a brat. "Of course I did. I'm sorry I left, but it felt like the old times, and the only thing I could do was fight or scramble."

"So you scrambled. That's okay. You didn't go far, and you talked to me. And you weren't gone for four months this time."

Such a brat but I didn't care. His hand was in my hair and his voice was husky and warm. "I'm getting better," I said.

"Yeah, you are."

Damnably, the lift stopped and the doors opened onto the foyer before the penthouse door. Jack was warily quiet as I led him in, which turned into what I desperately hoped was awed quiet as he took in the penthouse.

"Do you like it?" I tried not to hold my breath in anticipation.

"It's amazing. This is your place?"

Relieved and pleased, I chatted about the penthouse and Jack joked as he was wont to do. Then he had to revisit an incredibly sore spot, literally and figuratively.

"Is this was caused the bruises?" He ran the back of his hand over an old bump.

"It can be hard work sometimes." I had, after all, sustained an injury or two from working on the penthouse. "Do you like my surprise?"

"A lot." Jack cuddled me. "Do you want your surprise now?"

Daringly, I reached for his crotch. "Shall I get it for myself?"

Eyebrows arching high, Jack brushed me off then grabbed a phone from a back pocket. "How about I get it and you behave. Your surprise is on here. I hope you like it," he added tentatively. "I did some research this week and found this." He hit the screen.

Music started playing. I was certain I'd never heard it before, but it was tantalisingly familiar all the same. The melody sparked my recognition, but when the lyrics began, I was transported back to those very first memories I had. The voice on the phone—sweet and melodical—was different to the one in my head—off-tune, smoky, disinterested—but I latched on to it with frantic need. I could almost feel the soft hand on my head, the kisses she would shower on my cheeks when she felt happy or guilty. Could almost smell the mix of menthol and floral perfume. Hear her telling me she loved me, that I was a burden, a mistake, that I was her cherished boy and she would do anything for me. Had done everything for me.

Then the song ended and she faded again. In her place was the only person who'd ever truly cared for me.

"Was it the right one?" Jack asked gently.

I nodded.

"Was it—oh."

I threw my arms around his neck and held on for all I was worth. His arms went around me in return. "I guess it was good, then."

"Very good."

"I'm glad. It—"

I grabbed the front of Jack's shirt and dragged him over to the couch. It was now or never.

CHAPTER FOURTEEN

"I had planned to do this tonight, regardless. But later. Much later, when I'd worked up the courage." I removed my glasses and knelt between Jack's legs. "That was more than a lullaby. It was something I thought I'd lost so long ago. Thank you, Jack. It means . . . so much."

Jack shifted slightly, the movement outlining his thickening cock. "Ethan, you don't need—"

I stopped his words with two fingers on his lips. "I want to." I had been thinking about it for a while now, something I wanted to do to show Jack how much I trusted him. It was still frightening but not so much I couldn't go forward—but only if I was in complete control. "There will be some rules, though. No touching. Put your arms along the back of the couch."

Jack responded instantly to everything I asked with a seriousness that almost made me rescind the orders. He wouldn't hurt me. Still it took me a few deep breaths before I could touch him, and then to reassure myself he was here, that he was willing to do this for me. His thighs were tense under my hands, and his belly tightened when I caressed it, but he didn't move, didn't talk, although his gaze spoke volumes when I braved a quick glance. Care, concern, and desire all shone in his dark eyes, the brown irises catching highlights from the setting sun. He bit his lower lip as he watched my hands move over him and air caught in his throat when I grazed his crotch.

Inspired by his compliance, I undid his jeans and Jack lifted his hips to let me pull them down just enough. His cock strained at the soft cotton of his boxer-briefs and I freed it before I could think twice. This was easy. This I had done countless times before. I'd become extremely fond of watching Jack lose his mind when I handled him like this.

I stroked his hard shaft and considered getting him off this way. Jack wouldn't mind, I was certain of it. He didn't care how it happened, as long as it was me doing it to him. I knew it like I knew how to field strip and clean any firearm in the world.

My lips touched his cock without a conscious thought. Jack jerked, pulsing in my grip. I squeezed his balls and he squirmed, then settled. My heart had skipped a beat and now raced in remembered fear, but it swiftly reverted to desire. I kissed up his shaft, tasted the moisture at the tip, then explored the other side all the way down to his nest of black curls. The strangled sounds of Jack's excitement encouraged me, and I licked and kissed and probed with my tongue until he was biting his lips to keep from moaning aloud.

He was being so obedient that I felt calm and confident, so I sucked the head of his cock into my mouth. Jack nearly lost the fight to keep silent and the leather of the couch creaked under the pressure of his hands. I was doing this to Jack. I was in control and I was making him squirm in pure ecstasy.

I felt good. Not aroused but pleased that I could give this to Jack.

It couldn't have been the most elegant fellatio, or even very skilled, but it was enough to bring Jack to the brink. His breathing was fast and shallow and the quivering in his legs was nearly enough to vibrate the entire couch. Then he went still.

I looked up and was pinned by his dark gaze. In that moment there were no doubts. Jack was here, with me, for me, completely. He may have slept with Adam Quinn before we'd solidified our relationship, but it was me Jack had chosen to be with.

Jack came moments later. I hadn't planned to swallow but it happened naturally and wasn't as bad as I remembered. Perhaps that was more to do with who and how and why. However, the moment Jack slumped back with a satiated sigh and I let his cock slip out from between my lips, I had to move. It was instinctual and I let it carry me away from him, putting space between me and what had just happened. I got control back when I reached the large window overlooking Hyde Park. Glasses back on, I stared at the vista.

I couldn't pinpoint a singular feeling right then. There was a swirling mess in my head and another in my chest. I needed something solid to focus on, so I locked onto St. Mary's Cathedral. The setting sun bathed it in orange, bright points glinting off the very top of the twin spires. Slowly, the noise in my head quietened and I could start to process.

I'd overcome a long-borne fear, no small part of which was because of the man on the couch behind me, gently tucking himself away and zipping up. The trust I had in him, that he wouldn't force anything on me, was nothing I'd ever experienced before.

Without Jack I would never have that again.

"Thank you," he said. "It was amazing. Best ever."

Still a little unsettled, I nevertheless sent him a quick smile over my shoulder, acknowledging his reassurance. He was sprawled in the corner of the couch, watching me with half-lidded eyes and a sated expression. The urge to put my head in his lap and have his hand in my hair was strong. Lingering uncertainty kept me where I was. I turned back to the view. The lights were starting to come on in Hyde Park and the traffic turned into chains of white and red, twisting around the buildings like bindings holding them in place.

Jack stood and took a couple of steps towards me. "You know, I don't expect that all the time now. Or at all. It's entirely up to you, Ethan."

"I know."

"Good." Another tentative step. "Can I touch you?"

"Yes."

It was said without thought, but before I could question my instincts—or lack thereof when Jack was involved—he was there. Close but not pressing tight. He didn't hold me or push his face into my neck, his usual post-coital positions. He just stood with me, his chest barely brushing my back.

"God," he murmured after a while. "That's an awesome view."

"It's one of the reasons I bought this place."

Jack chuckled. "That, and it's very defensible."

The corner of my mouth turned up. "And that, yes."

We stood in silence until the sun finished setting and the view turned into a scattering of jewel-bright lights outlining the shapes of what was now invisible. Sometime during those passing moments, Jack's arms went around my waist and his chin settled on my shoulder.

I relaxed into him, all the doubts fading away at the simple joy of having him back with me.

Turning in the circle of his arms, I cupped his face in my hands and looked into his beautiful dark eyes.

"What?" He smiled cautiously.

"Thank you."

"For what?"

"For giving me exactly what I need."

Jack's smile faded and his expression twitched, like he was fighting some upwelling emotion. His arms tightened around me, his chest swelled, and his head tipped like he was going to kiss me . . . My heart thumped loudly, lips parting and . . .

Hands going to my arse, Jack smirked and squeezed playfully. "And right now, I think you need a return blowjob."

Surprise and relief made me laugh, which Jack took as agreement. Spinning me around, he faced me towards the bedroom and gave my rear a solid swat.

"Get in there and get naked."

"We will be having that discussion about this smacking penchant, Jack." Yet I was doing as instructed, loosening my clothes as I went.

"Yeah, yeah," he muttered, not far behind me. "We'll talk later. Much, *much* later."

Exhausted from the most pleasant exertions, I slept deeply, and by the time I woke up, Jack was gone. There was a note in his messy script saying he would be back after work. I lay in the massive bed for a long time, luxuriating in the knowledge that Jack would return.

Naturally, that was when Dejana called. She gave me a time and an address and requested that I provide the transport today.

I had enough time to dress, settling harness and weapons into place with a small twinge of regret. Things were moving forward with Jack again and the relief these small missions of Dejana's had given me wasn't there anymore. Even the threat of the Cabal felt more distant, but if she could ensure they'd never bother me again, then all the better.

I exchanged Victoria for the Monaro and arrived at the address Dejana gave me right on time. It was a bus stop in North Ryde and Dejana was waiting for me in a pale pink skirt-suit.

"Not exactly what I was expecting," she said dryly as she settled into the passenger seat.

"I thought it best to be inconspicuous."

She laughed when I slammed the huge V12 engine into gear and rocketed out in front of an oncoming bus.

"Where are we going?" I weaved through some traffic then slowed down and settled into a lane.

"Nowhere right now. Make sure we're not being followed."

As I roamed the streets of north Sydney, Dejana tapped at the screens of three different smart phones. She didn't say anything for half an hour, then started giving me directions. We headed eastwards and ended up at Balgowlah Heights, cruising along a scenic circuit.

"Here," Dejana said, pointing to a sign that said Arabanoo Lookout.

I pulled the Monaro over on the opposite side of the road, on the edge of a sports field. A team of teenaged footballers was training, with the attendant parents and vehicles. The Monaro didn't exactly disappear into a crowd of similar cars, but it stood out much less than Victoria would have. Cautioning Dejana to stay put until I gave the all clear, I got out and looked around. Our arrival had sparked no interest in the sports field population, and there were only a couple of people walking out to the lookout. There was, however, a lot of tree cover to either side of the path that didn't sit well with me.

"I don't like it," I reported softly when Dejana was standing beside me.

"I didn't pick it," she said just as quietly, smoothing down her skirt.

"Then why do this?"

She flashed me a tight smile. "Negotiations are all about give and take, Saint." Then she crossed the road and headed for the lookout.

By which I assumed she'd set up the last meeting, the one where she and Owen had been targeted by the gunman, so now she had to prove her good will by letting him pick the meeting point this time.

I followed several paces back, giving myself a clear line of sight all around her. There was no movement back in the vegetation other than the mild breeze that was coming off the water ahead of us. The walk was short and the lookout itself consisted of a couple of cement benches and a railing around the edge of the drop-off. Before us was a wide view of North Harbour and North and Middle Heads. The water was calm and blue, and a ferry cut across the surface like a blade leaving curled shavings in its wake.

Dejana went to the railing and looked out at the view. I maintained optimum distance. Around us, people came and went, none of them sparking my instincts.

Finally, Owen arrived. He was wearing jeans, football jersey, peak cap and sunglasses, but his body language screamed nervous tension. He gave a startled jerk when he saw me and skipped a couple of steps to the side to give me a wide berth.

"I said, no one else," Owen hissed when he reached Dejana, unintentionally loud by the way he then whipped around, looking for anyone who might have heard him.

"I think he's proved his worth," was Dejana's bland response before continuing in a much quieter voice. Her tone and words caught the young politician's attention and he focused his jumpy attention on her.

I stepped back another couple of paces, having absolutely no interest in whatever it was they were negotiating. From body language alone I knew it was something Dejana had that the man wanted, badly. And, eventually, it was something he got when Dejana dipped into a pocket and produced a data stick. He immediately snatched for it, but she held back, negotiating more. Nodding frantically, Owen pulled a phone out and made a hasty call. After a minute, he handed it over to Dejana, she spoke for a moment, then returned the phone. She then checked one of her own devices and, seemingly satisfied, offered him the stick.

As this was happening, I was aware of people coming and going from the lookout—and then only going. By the time the man had the data stick in his hand, we were the only ones there.

I was moving before a loud voice announced, "Australian Federal Police! Get down, get down!"

Dejana and Owen spun around. His mouth was open in shock as black-clad police appeared from the trees on both sides of the pathway. Dejana had no time to show a reaction because I caught her in a sweep of my arms and threw us both over the railing.

CHAPTER FIFTEEN

I rolled so I was on my back, Dejana on my chest. Spikey bushes broke our fall, though the hard rock underneath wasn't a pleasant aftermath. The AFP team advanced, yelling for us to stop and for Owen to get down. I didn't bother listening, instead tumbling again, taking us over the next little drop into the thicker vegetation below the rocky outcropping of the lookout. Dejana was thankfully silent except for involuntary gasps and yelps as the branches and bushes gave way under us in a staggering fall. Seconds later, we collected up against the trunk of a tree, solid ground beneath us.

A precautionary hand over Dejana's mouth, I listened. The AFP team was securing a now very vocal and indignant politician while the leader organised several of his officers to come after us. I doubted they would take the same, direct, route down, so we had a few moments to get further away.

Apart from a few spots that would bruise, I'd survived the tumble well enough, as had Dejana. As quickly and quietly as I could, I led her further downward, heading towards the water. We came across a walking trail and followed it, but back in the trees. Sure enough, two AFP officers appeared not long later, moving swiftly but alert and checking the trees on either side of the track. Dejana and I flattened ourselves in the undergrowth until they were well gone. We were making our cautious way back towards civilisation when my implant *ping*ed with a message from Nine.

Finally in Sydney.

Making sure we were secure, I stopped and called my sister.

"The navy is getting to be a real—"

"Where are you?" I cut off her opening diatribe. *"I could use some help."*

Her sigh was equal parts pained and resigned. *"Already? You're hopeless. I'm heading towards the bridge. Where are you?"*

I gave her a rapid report and she said she would get back in touch when she was closer. Dejana watched me the entire time, probably suspicious of my silence. I'd be very surprised if she was unaware of the existence of the neural implants, so I simply told her help was on the way and kept us moving.

We had another couple of close encounters with the AFP but eventually made it back to the edge of the bushland. When Nine got in touch, I sent her our coordinates and a minute later, she roared up on a white Suzuki.

"The things I do for you," she muttered as I handed over the keys for the Monaro.

I didn't bother reminding her of all the things I'd done for her. She knew very well the secrets I kept on her behalf. Still, she popped an obnoxious wheely as she took off.

"Is she like you?" Dejana asked when we were alone again.

I didn't answer and she just chuckled.

It was close to half an hour later before the yellow car cruised by and pulled into the driveway of a house across the street. Dejana and I strolled out of the trees and calmly got in. Nine had moved into the backseat, leaving me to drive. Which was preferable for both of us.

No one spoke as I took a very circuitous way back to the bus stop where I'd picked up Dejana.

"Thank you," she said when I pulled over.

"How much longer do you expect me to be at your beck and call?"

Dejana shrugged. "Depends on the fallout from today. I'll have another transaction completed by tomorrow." Then she got out and, straightening her torn jacket, walked away.

"She's blackmailing you?" Nine demanded as she scrambled over from the backseat.

Dodging an errant foot, I said, "Not exactly." I didn't want Nine to know what Dejana had promised me. If Zero asked her, she would tell him.

Nine snorted. "Sure sounded like it to me. She a facilitator?"

"And accountant." I slid the car back into the flow of traffic.

Eyebrows arched almost into her hairline, Nine said, "Accountant? You really are serious about going legit."

"I am."

That shut Nine up for a while. Then she told me where to go so she could pick up another bike. Once she was astride a red Suzuki, I gave her the address of the garage complex and she beat me there.

"Bit smaller than the last place," she observed when I opened the door and let her in.

"Suits my needs. I'm not living here this time."

She screwed her face up. "And how is married life?"

I threw a spare bolt at her. Nine dodged it without even looking.

"Have you offered yourself up to our psycho brother since we last talked?"

Resigned to her taunts, I told Nine everything about my interactions with Two and my estimation of why he was here. Nine peppered my report with her opinions, about him and me both, but at the end, she shook her head.

"You don't really think he's gone, do you?"

"I haven't heard from him in over a week."

Nine laughed. "So? Like that prick ever kept a promise." Then she got serious. "Look, either way, why would he care enough about your spy to set up such an elaborate scheme?"

"Because it's me he really wants to hurt."

"Bingo. I don't think the trap is for Loverboy at all."

"Then who? The profiler?"

With a loud groan, Nine stalked over and slapped the back of my head, calling me a few choice names in Afrikaans as she did so. "The trap's for you, and you've walked right into it."

Nine roared off on her new bike not long later, determined to find Two and "get answers." I wished her luck but also hoped he was already out of the country. When I got back to the penthouse, I took a long, hot shower and worked out the kinks caused by the tumble from the lookout. I'd have several new bruises by morning that I would have to somehow keep hidden from Jack. He wouldn't accept more excuses now the penthouse was finished.

Added to that worry was the one Nine had seeded.

If she was right and the trap was set for me, then Two had missed his mark. I knew Jack wasn't cheating on me. The road had been rocky, but we'd made it through all the curves and chicanes Two had thrown in our way. Jack and I were together and it would take more than a temptation from the past to break us up now.

Jack came in as I was running through a tai chi routine to help keep my abused muscles from tightening up. He joined me, not saying a word that I wore a T-shirt instead of going bare chested. We moved together in quiet synchronicity, exchanging small smiles when our gazes met. At the end, Jack caught me around the waist and kissed my neck and cheeks noisily, before all but dropping me and heading for the bathroom.

Washed and changed into jeans, he joined me at the dining table, making lip smacking sounds when I served up a simple dinner of rice and fish.

"I hope it's all right." I sat opposite and poked at the salmon. It was my first attempt at cooking the Spanish rice.

"It's brilliant." He hadn't even had a bite yet.

Amused, I muttered, "You must have had a hard day."

Swallowing his first mouthful with a swig of beer, Jack said, "Yeah. Things got official again today. The Judge killed another person last night."

No. Two had promised he wouldn't kill as the Judge again. "He did?"

"Woman. Twenty-three years old. He broke into her home and, *God*, he's just a sick fuck. The only good thing is it's made them start up Infinity again, and hopefully this time, they'll catch him. Hopefully in the crossfire."

"This wasn't supposed to happen." It was out before I could stop it.

"What?"

Jack's incredulous tone dashed my hopes he hadn't heard and I met his gaze for a moment. It was as if all the good things of the past twenty-four hours had never happened. We were right back to Jack being confused and angry, and all my lies were about to be exposed.

Two had broken his promise and I shouldn't have felt so betrayed by that, but I was for some unfathomable reason. Betrayed and devastated because I'd just fallen directly into Two's trap.

I stood and walked away.

"What did you say?" Jack demanded.

Locking everything down was automatic. I couldn't let Jack know about Two. He would only charge out into danger, looking for him, and that was a meeting that wouldn't end in Jack's favour. I wouldn't let Two get Jack.

"Do you know something? Ethan? What the hell did you say?"

"Nothing, Jack. It wasn't important. Just a random thought." If he believed it, perhaps I could as well.

"Don't lie to me, Ethan."

"Then I won't." Everything inside me hurt, like the fall had been a hundred times longer, the impact a thousand times harder.

Jack's persistence lasted longer than usual. He ranted at me for nearly half an hour but I was sealed away behind enough locks nothing got through. Until he said, "For fuck's sake, Ethan! This psycho is *killing* innocent people."

It was as if those reassurances Jack had given that the Judge and I weren't the same in his eyes had never happened. Doors opened and pain and fear leaked out. "Like I do, Jack?"

"Not anymore, right?" The doubt that turned the words into a question was blatant in his tone.

"Not anymore," I whispered even as I thought of the man I'd shot for Dejana. All I'd known about him was that he'd been reaching for a weapon. I didn't know why he'd been there, or who he'd been. There hadn't been time to find out, not with Two right beside me. There had been no choice.

Maybe I was just a murderer.

"Jesus Christ. I'm talking to an assassin about a serial killer. No wonder I don't understand what the hell you're saying."

It hurt like he'd stabbed me in the gut.

"Just tell me what you know, Blade. Or I walk out and don't come back."

Blade. Jack hadn't called me that seriously in so long it was like a slash across my heart. He was right, we were just knives waiting to cut anyone who got too close. Seemed neither of us had yet learned how not to hurt the other. But this was my fault. I'd been lying right from the start. If I'd just had the courage to tell Jack how I'd been feeling, then perhaps Two wouldn't have manoeuvred me exactly where he wanted me.

"Fine. I don't think I've left anything here. See you round, Blade."

I'd ruined everything and Jack was walking away, perhaps for the last time.

Two had to pay for what he'd done and since I'd proven I was incapable of stopping him, it was time for the Office to have a go.

"Look at them separately."

Jack turned slowly. "Pardon?"

Everything about my past that I'd wanted to keep as far away from Jack as possible crowded up against my back. "The victims. Look at them as two groups, not one." Unable to see anymore betrayal in his eyes, I let the mounting pressure of all those secrets and lies push me into the bedroom.

Jack and his fellow assets would work through the hint in no time and then the life I'd come to want so badly, to need with every fibre of my being, would be ripped away.

Just as Two had planned.

CHAPTER SIXTEEN

The steel security door was too heavy to truly slam, but Jack managed to close it with enough force I heard it in the bedroom. Even through the wild clamouring in my head. Even as it felt like my chest was cleaving in two.

I sank into a crouch, curling over my vulnerable spot, forehead to my knees.

Two had killed again as the Judge. He'd promised me he wouldn't, that he would leave Sydney and not bother me, or come after Jack, again.

I was a fool. A complete and utter fool.

I'd believed it to be the truth when I told Jack I'd quit dealing in death, but apparently the lying had started all the way back then. Stupidly, I hadn't realised how wrong I'd been and hadn't planned for anything that followed, and this was what it came to.

Me, here, unable to find order in the chaotic emotions, and Jack furious with me for lying to him, repeatedly. It didn't matter that I'd done it to protect him. He had every right to be angry.

Just twenty-four hours ago, everything had been perfect. Jack and I had been here, in this room. He had done more than give me a blowjob. He'd ravished me. Worshipped me. Devoured me. Every inch of my skin had been stroked, kissed, nuzzled and licked until I'd been a quivering mess.

That sort of affection survived arguments.

But could it survive everything that was going to be exposed when Jack worked out just how I'd lied to him? Would it survive him knowing about my past?

Would it survive Two's efforts to destroy it?

Even if it couldn't, it didn't change what I had to do now—make sure *Jack* survived whatever else Two may have planned.

Purpose anchored me. All the bleeding emotions could be locked away while I had a target to aim for.

The new injuries from that day made themselves known when I straightened up. I'd been curled over so long the strained and bruised muscles had stiffened. I was working them loose when my implant *ping*ed.

Hoping it was Nine with new information, I tapped the message and instantly knew it wasn't from my sister.

A video taken with an implant played, showing the interior of a stairwell. White walls, plain metal railing, and carpet on the steps. The footage was from Two's perspective—it couldn't be anyone else—who was walking with his head down, focused on the blue, red and yellow diamond pattern. A second set of footsteps came over the audio, fast and angry. The image shifted as Two turned his head away from the other man, but I caught a glimpse of his arm as they passed—red flannel sleeve and brown hand.

Jack.

My heart gave a single hard thump but I ruthlessly clamped down on the reactive fear.

The men passed each other without pause but when Two was on the next level down, he stopped and spoke.

"He told me about you."

Jack's footsteps halted and after a long moment, he said, "He told me about you, too." His tone was terse, the one he used when he really didn't want to engage.

I sucked in a sharp-edged breath. Jack knew Two?

"Do you want to know what he said about you? He said you're the only one who's ever made him happy."

I stopped breathing altogether. My words, in Two's mouth, and Jack couldn't know who Two was talking about.

"Sorry you had to hear that. See you round, Constable."

Constable?

Ice crystallised in my heart. Two had been much, *much* closer to Jack this entire time than I'd even suspected. Spying on him from within the police strike force. Manipulating Jack and Quinn for his own amusement. Undoubtedly tampering with evidence to keep them from linking him to the killer, as well.

Two had told me he'd taken a leaf from my book and *planned* the job out in detail. It just hadn't been the job he'd been sent to do.

The video was still playing while I realised how badly I'd misjudged Two, so I started it over and watched the rest.

"See you round, Constable," Jack said again.

"Are you going up there to fuck Adam?"

"What the hell? Where do you get off asking that? You kicked him aside, so it's none of your business."

Two had apparently gotten very close to the profiler.

"You already have a *boyfriend*." Two's voice dropped to a gravelly growl. "Are you a cheater, Jack?"

"Yeah. I'm going up there to make him *happy*. Good night, Constable." Jack's even angrier footsteps receded from the audio.

After a moment, Two continued on and I followed his process down the stairs, through a foyer and onto the street, where he turned and gave me a sterling view of the hotel where Quinn was staying.

It took me under fifteen minutes to reach the hotel. I knew I was possibly walking into a sight that may destroy me, but I had to do what I could to make sure Jack was safe.

The door to Quinn's room opened as I came out of the stairwell. Jack stepped out, his back to me, but stopped when Quinn spoke from within the room.

"I'm sorry, Nishant. I haven't had a great evening, in case you couldn't tell. Stay. Tell me what happened, and I'll try to be sympathetic."

His voice, so earnest and pleading, stopped me in my tracks. I didn't like that Quinn seemed so honest. Tired and honest. And I hated that it made Jack turn around and go back in. I stalked forwards, determined to stop whatever was going to happen in that room.

"We'd just got back together," Jack was saying as I reached the still open door and stopped just out of sight. "He left after you showed up at my place, said he wasn't safe there. I get it. I do, but he wouldn't let me go to him, either. But last night, he let me in, and now this."

There was a long silence, but I could hear someone moving around just inside the room and two sets of breathing became heavier.

I steeled myself against the sounds, against my imagination filling in the missing vision. Jack wouldn't be here if I hadn't driven him to it.

"Nishant," Quinn murmured. "He needs help, and maybe that help isn't *you*."

This time, I managed to lock down my gut instinct to hurt Quinn. It wasn't his fault I disliked psychiatrists and their biting insight and manipulative methods.

"You're just saying that because you want me for yourself."

"Probably." Quinn's tone turned smugly seductive. "But *you* came to *me*."

"To tell you about the case."

"You could have called. If you really wanted him over me, you would have stayed there. It was so good with us. It would be better now. What does he have that I don't? Apart from the obvious."

"My heart."

My heart leaped with Jack's words, then plummeted with Quinn's response.

"Does he? Have you kissed him on the mouth, Nishant? It's not hard to work out why you don't kiss like that. You have to love a person before you kiss them. You have to trust them with everything you are before you'll give them that final bit of your soul." Quinn's voice lowered and warmed. "I know you haven't kissed him. Does he know why, though?"

Not in those exact words, however I had suspected. The truth hurt like a bullet through my chest. I couldn't let it cripple me though, so I turned into the doorway. I had come for Jack and I would—

"Let me," Quinn whispered and kissed Jack's jaw.

The trap snapped shut.

I must have gasped, or whimpered, or screamed because Jack looked at me while Quinn pressed closer to him.

On some level I'd known what I would see, what Two had wanted me to see, but it still hurt. Only it wasn't Jack's knives slicing through me this time. It wasn't Two's. They were my own blades twisting inside me.

It was a wakeup call, in more ways than one.

There were things I wanted to say, needed to say.

"Jack, I'm sorry."

"Don't leave me, Jack."

"I love you, Jack."

Yet all I could focus on was how Two had manipulated us all, setting us in place so he could spring this trap.

Well, he wasn't the only one who could play that game.

Fixated on my new path, I said the only thing I could think of, "Turnabout is fair play, after all," and left before I could break completely.

CHAPTER SEVENTEEN

"**H**ave you found Two?" I asked Nine as I prowled the streets around the hotel.

It was entirely possible Two was still in the vicinity. Half, if not most, of the reason he messed with people like this was the enjoyment he got from seeing the chaos he created. He was the perpetual child, setting up the dominos just to watch them fall.

"*No,*" came the bitter reply a moment later. "*He just doesn't want to be found.*"

Which meant I would have to draw him out.

"Then leave it," I said. "*Best we concentrate on something we have a better chance of controlling.*"

"*Like what, the weather?*"

Not even Nine's dry humour could coax a smile out of me. "*I meant Jack's safety. I would very much appreciate it if you could keep a watch on him tonight.*"

Nine grumbled but accepted the address of the hotel. "*He better have a cute ass if I'm going to be staring at it for long.*"

It was both a long night, and far too short. Nine kept me updated about Jack's condition, though she quickly grew annoyed at his persistence in sulking in a park somewhere. I was, contrarily, quietly relieved he was at least *alone*, even if he was upset.

I spent the time clearing out both my storage shed and the rented garage while working through several plans for prying Two out of hiding. I moved Victoria to a new, secure place and used the Monaro. I'd already removed all of my belongings from the Leichhardt apartment and even if Two knew about the Bathurst penthouse, he wouldn't be able to get in there without destroying large sections of the walls.

It was clear now. The police tail I'd picked up on the way to the garage and the cop that had come asking about me had been Two, taking advantage of his cover to stalk me. To play with me. That was why Seven had been unable to find any official record.

And I hadn't worked it out until it was too late. Until Two had parcelled up his gifts and handed them to me.

It had barely been four months and already I was losing my skills. If I had any chance of beating Two at this game, I had to get back into top gear.

My burgeoning plans, however, were derailed just before dawn.

"Someone's bought a ticket on Loverboy," Nine reported, and my heart stuttered.

Finger curling around the trigger of a Desert Eagle, I asked, "Who?"

"Buyer's marked anonymous." As most of them were. *"Seven's looking into it."*

I must have made some dangerous noise because Nine hastily added, *"Eve Garrote's already picked it up. Don't worry. No half-assed amateur is going to accidentally kill him."*

Things were moving fast. The ticket was too coincidental to be anything other than Two's next step. With one unsanctioned death already on the job, Two would need to make any more official. Even if he had to buy the ticket himself.

The next update came barely an hour later.

"Loverboy just got arrested," she sent. *"Outside his apartment."*

I felt sick. "Is he all right?"

Nine snorted. *"He's fine. Went very peacefully. They picked him up on suspicion of murder."*

"Where are they taking him?" Already, the ill feeling was fading under a new calm. This was a situation I knew how to deal with. I would get Jack, put him somewhere very secure, and then go take care of Two. I had a plan ready to put into action the moment Jack was safe.

"Surry Hills LAC."

I stopped mid reach for the New South Wales police uniform I had in my stock of outfits, every inch of my skin prickling with a sudden dread. "Blast."

"What is it?" Nine demanded in my head. *"You don't trot out the bad language for nothing."*

I locked down my emotions. "You watched Jack all night. He didn't kill anyone, but clearly someone is dead."

Nine caught on quick. *"Two."*

"Indeed. And he's somehow managed to cast suspicion on Jack as well, so the victim has to be someone significant to Jack." The answer was obvious. "Two killed someone on the strike force." And there was one strong candidate for which one would make the police look at Jack. "Most likely Dr. Quinn."

There was a small silence from Nine, then without a trace of her usual sarcasm, she said, *"Sounds like him. So now what?"*

"I'll go fetch Jack. Could you contact Seven and ask her a huge favour for me?"

Nine groaned. *"How about I go get Loverboy and you do the impossible task for once?"*

She was right. On a good day, Seven wasn't easily swayed to doing favours. After the destruction of her safe place in Vietnam?

"Believe me, if I were to ask right now, it would be impossible," I assured Nine dryly.

"Ugh. Okay. What's the favour?"

I told her and suffered through the resultant rant while I changed clothes. By the time I was leaving my new storage unit for the LAC, Nine had wound down and promised to do her best.

Right now, against one of our own, it was all either of us could do.

Something bad had happened at the Surrey Hills LAC.

Jack had proudly told me how his demonstration had caused a sudden beef up on building security, but what I encountered was several steps beyond "beefed up." They had closed the doors to incoming civilians and posted well-armed guards on every ingress and egress point. My uniform and fake ID were perfect, but I couldn't take a chance that they wouldn't let me in without further authorisation. So I backtracked and found one of the ways into the Office's secret tunnels and came up through the basement carpark. Once that far past security, it was much easier to get into the main building.

They were holding Jack in a high-security interview room—the polite name didn't make it any less of an interrogation room—which, if it came down to it, I could break him out of with brute force. As could Two. Before making a move for Jack, though, I scouted the entire building. Making sure Two wasn't close to Jack was my main priority right then.

I needn't have worried. Two, or his police persona Constable Toomey, hadn't been seen since the day before. And Two wasn't someone easily missed, especially in a place he'd been moving about openly for several weeks. The more I listened to the whispers and gossip of the staff the less I worried for Jack's safety in the LAC. All of my lingering concern vanished the moment I gained access to the strike force's room on the second level.

Two would not be returning to the LAC. His plans for this place were complete.

They'd removed the body but nothing else in the room had been changed. The target had put up a fierce fight but unless they'd been trained to fight since early childhood, moves and countermoves ingrained into their very marrow, they would have had no chance against Two. He'd had to forego the Judge's usual MO, however, since this wasn't a private, empty building where he could take his time, so blood splattered the table and floor. It was smeared and streaked from the fight, but by far, the majority of it pooled on the table, where she had died.

And it was a she. Senior Sargent Stephanie Phelps. A single, blood-stained, pink sneaker, laces still tied, rested on its side under the table. A lady's small size.

Which meant the whispers I'd heard of someone else being missing were about Quinn. The leap to knowing Two had taken him wasn't a large one and I added finding the profiler to my list. I didn't like the man, but he didn't deserve to be subjected to Two.

Despite my wish otherwise, I was drawn to the board at the end of the room. It was filled with notes on the developing profile of the Judge. I read it thoroughly, even though the further I got, the less I wanted to know.

That was me on the board, described in Quinn's excited handwriting. How had Jack watched this profile take shape over the past weeks and not come to doubt me? Two's trap had been so detailed even I doubted my innocence after reading this. Jack's belief in me, his *trust*, was the only reason I wasn't under direct suspicion.

Assured Jack was as safe as he could be here until the Office came for him, I left by the same way I'd entered, free to continue with my plans for drawing Two out into the open.

"It's pretty obvious," Nine muttered once I'd explained it all to her that afternoon. She was in the passenger seat of the Monaro as we watched Jack's apartment building.

"Yes, but Two can't ignore it if he wants to continue his game." The coordinates and time I'd marked onto Jack's bathroom mirror were as far from subtle as I could get but disregarding a chance to use a trap for his own advantage would take an ego much smaller than Two's. "How long did Seven say it would take?"

Nine groaned. She's had some success with asking my favour of Seven, but it had been a hard slog, or so I'd gathered from the amount of swearing and moaning Nine had unloaded on me. "She said, and I quote, 'it'll take as long as it takes.'" Her monotonal recitation of the words were an exaggeration of Seven's usual tone, but not by much. "Until then, we're stuck here, waiting for our psycho brother to fall for a trap even Loverboy could spot from a mile off."

The immediate need to defend Jack didn't get past my drawing breath to speak. Across the street, Rocco Cesare came out of the building. His routine was to walk Short Round in the morning, before it got too hot, and then run errands in the afternoon. Except that this afternoon, he had Short Round with him. But what gripped my heart was that Shorty was cradled in Rocco's arms, little body limp.

"Hey." Nine's hand snapped closed around my wrist, stalling my unconscious reach for the door handle. "Where do you think you're going?"

"That's our neighbour," I began as a car pulled up to the footpath and Rocco headed for it.

"Oh." Even though her tone was understanding, her grip didn't slacken. "And there's a dog," she added wryly, knowing my soft spot for most animals.

We watched Rocco get into the car, tenderly holding Shorty to his chest. The moment he was in, the car pulled out and sped away.

"And there goes the dog," Nine murmured thoughtfully.

She was right, and I should have anticipated this turn of events. Another way in which I was failing. If Shorty was hurt or . . . worse, I would never forgive myself for missing his presence in the scenario.

Two hadn't missed it, obviously. He approached the building less than fifteen minutes later, wearing his police uniform. It would be the easiest way into the building, the clothes as camouflaging as the hat covering his hair and sunglasses hiding his eyes. Most people tended to avoid paying close attention to the person *in* the uniform, even someone of Two's extraordinary height.

I doubted that once inside he would let himself be seen getting into Jack's apartment, one reason why Shorty had to be removed from the equation. He'd already proven he could slip through my security measures and I hadn't changed them, except for a new camera placed in the bathroom with a view of the mirror and my "secret" message.

While Nine kept watch, I went *sideways* and called up the video feed through my implant. Sure enough, without setting off any of my alarms, Two appeared in the bathroom. He searched it efficiently but missed the camera tucked up into the slats of the ventilation fan over the shower stall. He didn't miss my message, though, steaming up the mirror and shaking his head as he read. The camera didn't have audio but I read his lips.

"See you there, One-three."

He left quickly.

"I don't know why we don't just kill the asshole now," Nine grumbled.

"Too many innocent people in the line of fire."

Nine shrugged but didn't say anything more.

We kept watch on Jack's place in shifts throughout the night. The moment he broke away from whatever restrictions the Office had put on him Jack would come home, probably looking for clues for my whereabouts. Likely, Two would come to the same conclusion and I couldn't trust he'd wait for the meeting at the Cenotaph the following night. As I watched the apartment block from my perch on the roof of the building across the street I replayed the call I'd received from Jack earlier.

"Blade, it's Jack Reardon. We have a situation we'd like your input on. Please make contact as soon as you can."

He sounded so formal it reminded me of those first interviews he had done when I'd been "captured" by the Office. Which meant someone had been listening to him dictate the message, explaining why he wasn't using his implant to contact me. Perhaps his tone was also covering his emotions. Did he hate me for the argument we'd had in the penthouse? Was he upset I'd interrupted whatever plans Quinn had for him?

Was he worried about me?

The first two had very little chance of being true, yet I could not stop them from circulating through my thoughts like poison in a vein. The last question was a small balm, because while I knew without a doubt it was true, it also made me want to tell Jack not to worry. To let him know that I was dealing with Two, that I was doing the one thing I knew how to do better than anything else, and that the only way I could do it was if I was certain he was safe.

The night passed peacefully, as did much of the next morning. Jack was still under lockdown with the Office and I allowed myself a small hope that he wouldn't fight them on it. Perhaps he had learned enough to know when to stay out of trouble.

It was a tiny hope and blown to even smaller fragments when Seven sent a message around lunch time.

"A second ticket was bought on the spy half an hour ago. Two's already picked it up, under the name Ethan Blade."

CHAPTER EIGHTEEN

knew exactly how Jack would feel knowing *Ethan Blade* had picked
up a ticket on him.

"Jack won't sit still now," I told Seven and Nine, the former
through the link we three had established, and the latter as she
strapped on a weapons harness. "Two knows using that name will
bring Jack out from cover."

Nine snorted as she secured her SIG into its holster. "Is Loverboy
that dumb he would really think you'd picked up a ticket on him?"

"Not dumb," Seven answered before I could. *"Confused and
hurting so he's angry enough he's not thinking straight."*

I stilled in tightening a nut on the new tyres I'd just put on the
Monaro and Nine turned slowly to face me, eyes wide and mouth
open in surprise. Seven might pick up subtle emotional cues, but she
never talked about them.

"Okay, and coming up next on Dr. Phil," Nine said dryly.

Before one sister could provoke the other into refusing her
assistance, I said, "Seven, have you had any luck with your other
project?"

Nine stuck her tongue out at me but went back to sliding weapons
into various concealed places about her person. I finished with the
tyre.

"I'm close," Seven said. *"Perhaps another hour or so."*

"Blast. We'll have to do our best to track him physically," I said to
Nine.

Doing up her leather jacket, Nine smiled, all teeth and predator.
"No worries." She slung her leg over the red bike.

"Keep us updated," I said to Seven as I got into the car.

"Will do."

The moment the door was open, Nine shot out on the bike, startling a couple who were unloading a trailer full of furniture into the storage shed across the way. They were still staring after her when I gunned the Monaro's huge engine, making them jump again. Unlike my sister, I eased the car out of the shed, letting the massive rumble of its twelve cylinders override everything else.

My worries and circling thoughts couldn't be heard over the beautiful noise of a finely tuned engine. Just to chase them further away, I stopped at the gates of the storage facility and, when a gap appeared in the traffic, floored the accelerator and rocketed the Monaro out onto the road. Back end swinging out, she nevertheless responded well and, rear tyres smoking, I charged into battle.

Pity we didn't find one for a while, and when Seven finally *ping*ed success with the favour I'd had Nine beg of her, I was nowhere near where it would go down.

"Cabal tracking system finally hacked," Seven reported. *"GPS location for Two coming in now."*

Sure enough, my overlay lit up with a map of Sydney and a red dot flashed, indicating Two's position.

The Cabal could track us through the implants, but we had never been allowed such access to each other. Any time we'd been required to know where our siblings were, it had been facilitated by the Cabal. Except not anymore.

"I'm about ten minutes away from him," Nine sent.

"Go. I'm twenty minutes out," I replied. The car was a hinderance in the city traffic, but if Jack was injured I'd rather get him away easily, and relatively more protected, than not.

As we worked our way towards Two's position, Seven kept us updated.

"Shots fired. Police response five minutes out."

"Nearly there," Nine reported, deadly serious.

"Don't close with him," I commanded, even as Seven echoed me word for word.

Nine just laughed.

She didn't make it in time to even have a chance.

"*Damn it*," she growled over the link a couple of minutes later. "*Two's gone and Loverboy's about to take off.*"

"Follow Jack. I'll take Two." I pushed aside the burst of relief at knowing Jack was well enough to ride. A meeting with Two could have gone much worse.

Two had to be on a bike, the way his tracking dot moved along streets I was having trouble navigating swiftly barely a minute later. I kept on his tail, however, hoping that he might lead me to wherever he was keeping Quinn. If the man was still alive. It all depended on Two's intentions.

I was finally starting to close the distance between us as we headed out of the inner city and into the northern suburbs when the tracking dot vanished from my overlay.

"Seven? What's happened?"

"*They killed his implant.*"

I nearly drove into the rear end of a bus.

Nine's shocked "*What the—*" devolved into a lot of swearing in Afrikaans.

The Office had given Jack the option of disabling his own implant when he joined them, and I knew he was mostly autonomous in his use of it. I suspected the Office would have the ability to override the implant, but only in dire circumstances. We Cabal assassins, however, weren't given any such consideration. Our handler, Zero, could and did access our implants whenever he wished. As could the core leaders. Anything stored on the implants was theirs to see and do with as they wished. Any use we put them to was logged and studied. The Cabal could in turn send location pings at any time to find out where we were—as Seven had been doing with Two.

I had never known that they could kill our implants remotely, however.

"*They discovered my hack,*" Seven responded coolly. "*Killing his implant was the only way they could stop me tracking him.*"

"Do they know it was you?" I asked grimly.

"*No. They're not good enough to do that. They weren't even good enough to kick me out of their systems.*"

Thus why they took the drastic action they did. Because now, not only could we not follow Two, the Cabal had absolutely no control on him at all—except for the conditioning they had indoctrinated into us, and we had all tested that upon occasion in the past.

"This is not good," I muttered.

Nine snickered. *"Because it's all been roses up till now. Oh shit!"*

"What?" I demanded.

"Fucking truck tried to drive me off the road. And great, Loverboy's disappeared into traffic."

My pulse stuttered. This was a fine time for Jack to manage to lose Nine. "Keep trying to find him, please."

Nine snorted and was silent, apparently concentrating on the search for my errant man.

While Seven started on hacking into Sydney's traffic systems in a hope of catching sight of Two that way, I continued a rather aimless search of the area Two had led me into. It was clear I was wasting petrol and the only chance I had of finding Two again was if Seven found him on a traffic camera.

Then Dejana called.

I'd routed the phone she'd given me through my implant and I seriously considered not answering, but I doubted this was a social call.

"Hello."

"I need you." She didn't sound particularly alarmed.

"I'm busy."

"And I have an AFP team closing in on me. If you don't wish me to tell them how you aided me in escaping them last time, I suggest you help me now."

As Jack would say, I knew this was going to come back and bite me in the arse. If she was caught, not only would she not be able to sever me from the Cabal, but Director Tan would undoubtedly learn of my activities through the AFP, and that would void his agreement with Jack and I would be an open target for the Office once more.

"Where are you?"

She gave me the address and hung up.

Blast it all.

I braked hard halfway through an intersection and threw the Monaro into a sharp turn. Drivers honked, yelled and gave me the finger out the window, but I was gone in a squeal of tyres and curl of smoke. The huge engine roared as we tore down another street. The address Dejana had given me was not far from where I'd picked her up the other day, and I was already very close to the location, so I was there within ten minutes.

Dejana wasn't.

I lapped the block and when I came past again, I saw her dart between parked cars and wave discretely.

Discretion was long gone, so I slammed the car to a halt and threw open the passenger door. She dived in and we were away before the door was even closed. As we took a corner fast enough to have Dejana clutching at the door and dash, a large, dark-coloured SUV swung in behind us. It was unmarked, but even if they'd put a large sign on the bonnet saying AFP, they couldn't have been any more obvious.

I floored the accelerator and weaved around the cars in front. A red light started flashing in the rear vision mirror as the SUV surged after us. Seeing the light and hearing the siren, civilian cars scattered out of the way of the police, but not as quickly as I was manoeuvring around them.

It wasn't a fast chase with the amount of traffic but it took skill to keep moving. Dejana sank low into her seat, bracing against a lot of rapid turns and sudden swerves.

Ahead I spied an arterial road and made a sharp right to get onto it, only to slam on the brakes. Another AFP SUV barrelled towards us in the middle of the road, lights and sirens allowing them to barge through the traffic.

Dejana spat something in a language that sounded eastern European, then gasped as I rammed the Monaro into reverse and rocketed us backwards out of the trap. The police that had been behind us had just reached the intersection and angled across it to block our escape. I threw the car into a breakneck reverse one-eighty, the nose of the Monaro clearing the side of the SUV by inches. We came to a shuddering stop parallel to the SUV. With only a narrow space between the back of the SUV and the refuge island in the middle of the road, and the second AFP car coming into the intersection, it appeared that there was nowhere for us to go.

"Saint," Dejana said warningly.

"This isn't a problem."

I waited until the second SUV had come to a stop, then put the car into first and hit the accelerator. The V12 engine exploded into full roar. When I released the clutch the whole car lurched, then I stood on the brake and the drive wheels started spinning in place. Smoke bloomed around the rear of the car, the stench of burning rubber quickly infiltrating the interior of the Monaro. There was movement inside the SUV beside us but no cops emerged, probably wary of entering a situation where they were visually compromised— my precise intent.

"One-three, I've found Loverboy again," Nine said inside my head. *"He's running east—"*

I blocked the link between myself and my sisters, needing to concentrate on the moment right now. It was a comfort knowing Nine was back in sight of Jack, but until I got out of the current mess, it wasn't something I could linger on. So I didn't.

Calmly, I let the tyres spin against the asphalt until the entire car was wreathed in smoke thick enough I couldn't even see the SUV outside my window. There may have been shouts from the federal police but the sheer avalanche of sound from the Monaro drowned it out to the point it may as well have not existed.

"Saint?" Dejana had to yell over the noise.

"Hold on," I said.

She tightened her grip on the seat and pressed back into the leather even further.

Judging it time, I ceased the burn-out, rapidly shifted into reverse, and floored the accelerator.

We burst out of the covering smoke backwards, swerved around the second AFP SUV and roared down the arterial road I'd initially wanted to take, facing the wrong way. Thanks to the blockade at the intersection, the lane was empty and I let the Monaro fly. We were several blocks away and starting to encounter traffic again when I slowed, and in a clear spot whipped the car around, bounced over a centre island and took another side street. There was no sign of pursuit. Yet.

I spent a good while making sure we didn't pick up any more tails and keeping an eye out for a car I could steal. Staying in the Monaro wouldn't do us any good now that the AFP had had a good look at it.

My eye was on a new silver Ford Mustang when I opened up the link to Nine and Seven again.

"I'm back," I sent silently. *"What's happening?"*

"Where the hell have you been?" Nine continued before I could even think about answering. *"Loverboy's not very smart, is he? He thought he was very clever evading me, but then he rode straight into a police blockade."*

"Is he all right?" Alarm tried to break through but I pushed it aside. Jack needed me clear headed.

"For now," Nine muttered. *"They've got him in the back of a car while they try to decide what to do with the arsenal he was riding with. He had a P90."* That seemed to impress her.

This wasn't good. If Jack ended up back in police custody, he would be a sitting target again, and I doubted the authorities would let him go so easily this time.

"We have to get him out of there," I sent. *"Where are they?"*

Thankfully Nine didn't argue with me and as I headed for her, we worked out a quick and dirty plan. When we reached the scene, I stopped the car well back from the intersection at the bottom of the off ramp from the highway. The red Suzuki motorbike pulled up beside the Monaro moments later. Nine and I surveyed the situation, refined our plan and when it was done, I eased the car forward and into the intersection.

The police were too busy cataloguing the weapons Jack had been carrying to notice the car, so I revved the engine. That got their attention. I revved it again, longer and harder. The whole car vibrated around us. One of the police officers gave orders to the others, then started to approach, one hand on his gun, the other held up as if he could stop me physically. I let the Monaro answer his demand.

"What are you doing?" Dejana asked.

"Finishing what I started before you interrupted me."

She was quiet for a moment then said, "If you get me to my exit point by eight p.m. I'll transfer the rest of your money free of charge."

At this stage getting my money was the least of my worries. "And you will facilitate my complete severance from the Cabal." It wasn't a question.

"Yes."

I nodded. "Good. Now get into the backseat and stay down."

Dejana gave me a wide-eyed look but clambered into the back. "Now what?"

"Brace yourself. This is going to be fun."

CHAPTER NINETEEN

Driving calmed me. Driving fast around a racetrack centred me as few other things could. Driving fast while dodging traffic and evading dogged pursuit was pure bliss. The decisions were immediate, the moves ingrained in muscle memory, everything was physics and mechanics and spatial cognition. It didn't need emotion or personal awareness. It was simple.

And it was definitely fun.

Six of the cops took the bait and followed us in three cars, leaving behind only two officers and the car holding Jack for Nine to deal with. Easy odds for her. The strength of the pursuit, which came to include two more cars as we raced westwards on the highway, had to be thanks to our earlier encounter with the AFP. They had undoubtedly given the description of the Monaro to the city police, who took the chase very seriously.

So seriously, in fact, it took me a good hour to shake them long enough for us to ditch the Monaro in an empty industrial yard, set it on fire, steal a mid-sized SUV, and drive sedately away like any other law-abiding citizens.

All the while, Dejana's only concern was the time it ate up. Her exit point was a small, private airstrip just west of Wollongong, nearly two hours drive south of Sydney. It would be tight, but I was certain we would make it in time. She wasn't the only one with a deadline tonight.

Nine sent a message that Jack was safely away from the police and, at her best judgement, back within the security of the Office. She ended it with the observation, *"Great ass and some okay moves, but he's not very bright, is he?"*

We ditched the second stolen car of the day—an old Honda hatchback—a couple of blocks away from the new storage unit and walked the rest of the way. I wasn't worried that it would lead the police here. After tonight, I wouldn't need it anymore. One way or another.

"Now this," Dejana murmured appreciatively when she saw Victoria, "is the style I expected from you, Saint." She ran a hand along the smooth lines of the Vanquish and made a low humming sound in the back of her throat.

"I'm glad you approve. Get in, we don't have much time to spare."

The drive out of Sydney was tedious thanks to evening traffic, but when we hit the highway going south, Victoria got to unleash herself on a much more open road. The Monaro had performed amazingly and I would miss it somewhat, but nothing beat the pure symphony of a finely crafted, high-powered supercar. Even Dejana melted into the leather seat and sighed contentedly.

We encountered no obstacles and drove through the gates of the airfield with three minutes to spare. A small twin prop plane was on the tarmac, propellers spinning.

"Thank you, Saint," Dejana said as she opened Victoria's door. "I do appreciate everything you've done for me over the past weeks."

I acknowledged her sincerity with a nod. "How long will it take you to do what you promised?"

Dejana opened her mouth, then shut it and after a moment shrugged. "I've never had to facilitate something so unusual. It can be done. I have . . . leverage with certain elements involved. It may take a month, maybe several. I'll let you know when it's done by transferring the money from the final Swiss account. The rest of your transfers were finished this morning, free of charge."

"Thank you."

She got out and walked over to the waiting plane. Once she was safely inside and the plane's engine was winding up further in preparation for take-off, I backed Victoria off the tarmac, turned and left the airstrip.

If I pushed the speed limits on the way back to Sydney, I would make it in time to catch Two at the Cenotaph before Jack.

I didn't make it.

Nothing more sinister than the usual Sydney traffic evils held me up, but it was enough.

"Where are you?" Nine demanded right on ten p.m.

"Nearly there," I ground out, swerving around a lumbering truck.

"Doesn't matter, you're too late." She heaved a sigh. *"Loverboy's winging it. Like I said, not very bright."*

"I'll be there in five minutes. Please, do what you can to keep Two away from Jack."

Nine groaned. *"You owe me peppermint crisp tart every week for the rest of your life."*

"Done." All things considered, it was an easy promise to make.

Five minutes later, idling on Pitt Street, I could see things hadn't gone according to plan. A pair of shadowed figures fought close by the dark bulk of the war memorial. They were unmistakably Nine and Two. I couldn't see Jack anywhere and hoped he was well away from danger but didn't bank on it. That wasn't Jack's standard operating procedure at all.

Spinning Victoria's steering wheel, I turned directly into the pedestrian mall and floored it.

At the Cenotaph, Nine delivered a powerful kick to the back of Two's knee. He buckled but turned it into a roll and came up on his feet. Only to jerk back, the faint echo a gunshot barely audible over Victoria's roar. Jack stepped out of the shadows by the Cenotaph, gun up—and right into Victoria's path toward Two.

Thankfully, Jack dived out of the way as I slammed her into handbrake turn, aiming for Two. Her rear fender hit him with a satisfying thump and he flew backwards, hitting the ground hard. Hopefully it was enough of an advantage for Nine to get the upper hand.

Leaning over, I opened the passenger door. "Jack! Get in."

"We need to secure Toomey." Jack prowled around Victoria, heading for the spot Two had been, USP up and ready.

"Jack, leave him." My plan had failed but I wasn't about to let Jack risk himself unnecessarily. "Nine will take care of him. Let's go."

The stubborn oaf hesitated, then continued on. "Toomey! Drop your weapons and show me your hands."

Some days, I thought Jack's sheer contrariness would drive me insane. I opened my door and, using it as a shield, covered the area around the Cenotaph with an Eagle. "Jack. Leave it. Get in the car."

"Yes, Jack," Two said teasingly from his hiding spot. "Best you do as the little woman says and get in the car."

I was used to Two's provocations. Jack was not.

Growling, Jack said, "I'm taking you in, Toomey. You're going to tell me where Adam is."

"No." Two revealed himself and my heart leaped into my throat. "You're going to leave, or I break her neck."

He had an arm around Nine's neck, hand holding one side of her face. The other gripped her shoulder. Nine didn't move, completely aware of how easy it would be for him to end her life.

"Nine," I said aloud, but sent silently, *"On three,"* and aimed for my brother's head.

"Don't close with him," our sister sent, even as she said, "My fault, One-three. Get out of—"

The snap of Nine's neck was like a bomb detonating. Everything went white and hot and a deafening roar ripped through me. I squeezed the trigger and the roar became the gunshots, became me screaming just to vent the fire searing my blood and brain, burning away the locks I had put on my emotions. All of the frustrations and fears of the past days flooded my body.

I had never used a weapon with intent to kill one my siblings. Not even when my own life had depended on it.

I couldn't stop firing at my brother as he ducked behind the cover of the Cenotaph.

"Ethan, let's go."

Jack.

Jack was here.

Nine was gone, but Jack was here.

The desire to chase Two, to make him hurt and cry, was strong, but I took my finger off the trigger and got back into the car. My hands were trembling with the need to hold a gun, a weapon of any sort, so I curled them around the steering wheel, wanting the calm I usually found there. It didn't work.

Jack got in, at last and too late, and I slammed the gearstick into reverse and hit the accelerator.

Everything blurred and not because of the speed. I acted on muscle memory and instinct until we hit George Street and I had to focus on the cars around us.

The plan had failed and Nine had paid for it with her life. She had been my sister, my only true companion in this life. Now it was just me.

"Where are we going?"

I wasn't alone, though. Jack was here and he would do everything he could to bring Two in. And yet, it wouldn't be enough.

"The last safe place I know."

At least this time when I surrendered to the Office, they didn't drug me. They took all my weapons, but Jack's director, Donna McIntosh, protected Victoria from being pulled apart at least. Instead of a subterranean cell, they took us to a meeting room several flights aboveground.

And I told a pair of Office directors, Jack, and his friend Lewis everything about Two's presence in Sydney. The words felt sharp and deadly as they came out, leaving me raw inside. Open and hollow. Jack's presence helped greatly. These were people he trusted, and I trusted him. I left out Dejana and what I'd done for her. That was a conversation best left for a time when she was well out of the country and had fulfilled her promise of severing the Cabal's hold on me for good.

Finally, enough figurative blood was spilled to satisfy the directors, for now, and they left to debate their next step. Lewis lingered for a moment, but grudgingly departed at an unsubtle hint from Jack. Which left us alone for what felt like the first time in a very long time, not just two days. I wanted to touch him, hold him, assure myself he was whole and safe. I distracted myself by pacing around the large table.

"Is this room secure?"

"Yeah," Jack said from his seat, "but monitored. They'll have a record of everything we do in here." His tone was even but I felt his reciprocal need in the words all the same.

Everything was exposed now. Not that the Office hadn't been aware of our relationship before, but the polite veneer of pretending they didn't was gone. And everything hurt so much I simply needed to be in his arms.

"I don't care."

Jack stood and caught me as I hurled myself at him. His strong arms wound around me and soaked me in warmth and strength and what felt like love. I finally let myself think about what I'd overheard Quinn say that night.

"Have you kissed him on the mouth, Nishant? It's not hard to work out why you don't kiss like that. You have to love a person before you kiss them."

The realisation that he was right still hurt. I let the pain roll through me, alongside that of Nine's death, of Two's actions, of everything the Cabal had done to me over the years. Compared to those hurts, to the comforting weight and encompassing warmth of his arms around me now, holding on tight and desperate, that pain was nothing. Maybe Jack didn't quite love me the way I loved him, but what he did feel, what he could give me, wasn't nothing either.

We talked briefly about Quinn and my reactions to him, and how helpless I felt trying to deal with the emotions his presence sparked. Jack murmured warm assurances, then asked if I would see a psychiatrist. It was only his offer to accompany me that let me agree, even if it didn't quench the nausea the prospect sparked.

Perhaps in an attempt to delay more discussion about psychiatrists, I was far more honest than I had ever been before. I didn't feel entirely secure, even within one of the Office's buildings, but it finally needed to be said plainly.

"Two was both my worst tormentor and my protector." I had never said these things aloud before and the words were sharp against my already raw throat and heart. And yet, as they kept spilling out, I felt lighter somehow. "He could be charming and sweet, which made his attacks so much worse. I was lost and scared. All I knew was sometimes, he would pick me up and hold me, tell me he wouldn't let anyone else touch me, and I believed him. Every time. Then he would cut me, or try to burn me, or leave me at the mercy of the others."

Jack's reactions as I continued told me that I was right. He did love me in his own way. Especially when he held my scarred foot so gently while his face and words were drenched in anger toward those who let it happen.

"And Two?" Barely contained rage made his voice low and rough. "Was he punished?"

Jack still clung to his ingrained sense of right and wrong. "What for? I was the weak one."

"Jesus fucking shit. Ethan—" He cut himself off before he exploded.

I had dreaded Jack finding out about my past, hated the possibility that it might change the way he felt about me. The fact that it was showing me how deeply he did care for me, love me, was too much for me right then as well. Too much for either of us while Two was still out there, hopefully keeping Quinn alive as bait for another trap.

"I survived, Jack, and I'm here now. Not quite right, but getting better." I touched his arm to make him look at me. "And I may know where Two has Adam."

CHAPTER TWENTY

We left the building without anyone interfering. Director McIntosh had been true to her word and no one had touched Victoria, or the weapons she carried.

I told Jack what Two had said to me about the special place he went to 'think and cry.' He thought about it for a moment, then gave me directions to Middle Head. As we kitted out with weapons, I explained about Two's eyes. They were his only weakness even though it would be hard to exploit in the middle of the night.

Jack took us along a walking trail away from the main path. We worked our slow, methodical way through the old gun placements, clearing each one before moving on. I kept lookout while Jack searched the ruins. While my eyes scanned the surrounding trees, my mind scanned over everything that had happened in the meeting room, everything that had happened over the past days and weeks and months since I'd met Jack.

I glanced down into the gun emplacement he was scouting and was struck anew by how he made me feel. Not just the *types* of emotions he inspired—because he sparked them all in me, lust, joy, fear, anger, contentment, love—but the simple fact that *he* made me feel *anything* at all.

I would fight for that until all the blood was gone from my body. I would fight for him. For us.

The gun emplacements proved to be empty so we moved onto the main ruins at the end of the peninsula. Jack was disappointed that we hadn't found Quinn or Two yet and as we stood there, silently trying to work out what our next move was, I saw him make a decision.

Jack came to my side and whispered, "I think I know where they are."

This park meant something to Jack. Something deep and personal, and yet, there was more hurt behind his dark eyes as he spoke now. I connected with the pain in his voice, with the sudden tension in his body, as if he could see the knife poised before him and knew he had to throw himself on it. My heart ached for him.

"All right. Tell me."

"They're called tiger cages. They trained soldiers to resist torture in them."

Each word was an acceptance of the knife and the damage it would cause, and a resistance as well.

"Are they otherwise significant to you?" I prompted.

"Yeah." Jack swallowed hard. "I brought Dad here once, after he got sick. I hoped it would help him remember good times. He found the tiger cages and told me that, when I was lost in India, he imagined I was in a cage, being tortured. And he hoped that I was dead instead."

The roughness of his voice echoed my own from the meeting room. I doubted Jack had ever said these things aloud before. He was cutting himself open before me, letting me see his most inner scars. The trust he was giving me was immense.

I wanted to hold him, tell him I loved him, but this wasn't the time or place. I could protect him from more pain, however. "I'm sorry. But I think you're right. Two will have worked out that area is painful for you. Tell me where it is, and I'll go alone."

Jack shook his head and firmed up his voice. "We go together."

Another line of Quinn's from that night played across my mind as Jack spoke.

"You have to trust them with everything you are before you'll give them that final bit of your soul."

It all fell into place at long last. Every last puzzle piece that was this beautiful, amazing, infuriating, *stubborn* man before me slotted into perfect alignment.

Jack was scared. Everyone he'd loved had left him, whether they were taken by death, ideological differences, a cruel disease, or hadn't resisted when Jack pushed out of fear. He'd isolated himself. Stopped living. And yet he'd let me—his enemy—in. He'd let me pick his locks one by one and steal into his work, his house, his bed—his trust.

Jack shifted nervously. "What?"

In that moment I didn't care that Two might be stalking up behind me. Or that we weren't safe behind a dozen locks and alarms. None of it mattered when Jack was looking at me with that gorgeously quizzical and worried frown.

"I want you to know, Jack, that I don't care about whatever happened between you and Adam. I lied to you. I should never have done that. If I hadn't, we wouldn't be here now and Adam wouldn't be in danger. I'm sorry, Jack."

"Me too. About Adam—"

"I don't care," I reiterated. "I heard you and him talking. I was there for longer than you thought I was."

Jack's frown deepened. "Shit."

I moved our weapons to the side and got closer to him. This was something I had to do now, while I had the courage and before we faced the most able assassin the Cabal had ever fielded. It felt right but that didn't mean Jack was feeling the same way.

"I understand, Jack, I do. Considering everything I've done to you, it's reasonable. But I want you to know, before we find Two and possibly not survive, that I . . ." This was it. Would Jack push or pull? "That I . . . Oh, blast it."

I kissed him. On the mouth.

It was . . . one-sided. I pressed my lips to his, feeling his shocked gasp, then nothing as he froze. But he didn't pull away. Didn't turn his head or push me back. Just stood there and let me kiss him. It wasn't a rejection. It was trust. He trusted me to be the one to do this for him. For us.

Then he kissed me back and I was tumbling wildly within the tight hold of his arms. I couldn't feel my feet or the top of my head. The only parts of me that were real and solid were those he was touching. My waist, back, chest, arms, lips. The rest of me was incidental, shrapnel from the explosion of Jack kissing me. Every moment of pain and laughter and comfort was encapsulated in that one long and far too short moment. It hurt and it healed and when it ended, it felt like a new beginning.

"Just so you know," I whispered. And then because only the promise of Two's inevitable cruelty was never far away, I pulled back and hefted my Assassin X rifle. "Shall we get on with this?"

Jack's somewhat dazed confusion made me want to kiss him all over again. "Sure." He got himself together quickly, though, and followed me towards the tiger cages.

The plan we made was simple. I would draw Two out, Jack would try to flank him in secret, and we would catch him between us.

"He doesn't seem the sort of fall easily into a trap," Jack whispered just before we parted ways.

"He isn't. But I believe I can provoke him."

Jack's teeth flashed in a quick grin. "If anyone can, you can." Then he melted into the darkness and I already missed his solidity.

Trusting Jack to keep pace as I went openly and he in secret, I approached the tiger cages. Two was surely expecting one, or both, of us, so I moved cautiously but not silently. The area was open and Two would doubtless see me coming. He'd let me get to the position he wanted me in, then spring his final trap.

Adam, however, spoiled Two's surprise when he coughed, ragged and painful, the sound rising from the sunken entrance to the cages.

"Oh shoot," Two said from somewhere in the trees. "There goes the surprise."

"You overestimate yourself, brother. We knew exactly where you were."

"Hey? Help!" Adam rasped. He was below my current position, most likely in the subterranean cages.

"Quiet, lover." Two sounded amused, but I heard the hitch on the last word.

That was how I was going to provoke him into being careless. It was one thing Two and I had in common—we'd never been interested in sex. It was a tool to be used when required, that's all. I had changed my mind since meeting Jack, but for Two, it was like crawling through mud to reach a target—dirty, wet, disgusting, and purely a means to an end.

"Shut up, Quinn." I feigned disinterest in him but hoped he got the message to keep quiet. "I'm not here for you. I'm after *him*."

"But," Quinn tried and both Two and I drowned him out with "Shut up." Our synchronicity made Two laugh, which helped me pinpoint him on the far side of the ruins beyond the tiger cages.

"I've missed you, One-three," he said pleasantly. "We used to have some fun times together."

I moved slowly toward Two's position. "Yes. It was fun when you broke my ribs when I was nine."

"It taught you to watch your six, didn't it?" Two moved within the trees. "I made you the man you are, baby brother."

It was the "baby brother" that rankled me. Brothers didn't do what he did to me.

"You made me a monster, Two." I had his position fixed, and Jack's. Deliberately, I angled towards Jack, to make Two think I was off mark. It was time to draw him out. "Jack made me a man."

Adam gasped in surprise, but it was the vicious snarl from Two that I concentrated on. Yes, he was to my left, but moving now, towards Jack. I tracked him, shifted ahead of his trajectory and fired. Close to Jack to hopefully misdirect Two away from him.

"You used to be a better shot," Two taunted, and he wasn't where I thought he was, still back on my left flank. "Maybe you should be a monster again, instead of letting that prick corrupt you."

"But the way he *corrupts* me. So much better than anything you ever did to me."

"Do you know he's a cheater?" There was a tremor to the words, faint but clear to anyone who had lived with him for the first half of their life. "He fucks other men while you're at home waiting for him."

It was working. Another shove and he would make a mistake. I had to say something extra provocative. "I don't care about that, because it feels so good when he's inside me." Normally, I would have cringed at saying something so raw and blatant, but this was just part of the game. "When he comes and I feel his hot spunk flood my guts." I could practically sense Two vibrating with a need to deny and challenge. "I let him take me from behind so I can't see him. So I'm vulnerable. I don't care about my six when he's pumping into me. All I know is how deep he—"

Two screamed in rage and flew into motion. But the sounds came from different directions and I realised my mistake. He was using speakers to misdirect us. I focused on the violent rustling of foliage and not the growls. Two was right on top of Jack! Then he hit and they crashed to the ground.

The sound of a sharp snap froze me in place. "Jack?"

I only realised I'd spoke aloud when Quinn demanded, "What? What's happening?" It broke me out of visions of Nine going limp in Two's arms and I rushed forwards, rifle at the ready.

Jack emerged from the trees and relief sparked. Then I saw the arm around his neck and the tall figure pressed to his back. Two kept Jack between him and my weapon. Below, Adam moaned a despairing curse.

Too close. It was too close to what had happened with Nine. I was done playing. I couldn't lose Jack as well as my sister in one foul night.

"Let him go, Two. I'll go with you if you do." It was what he wanted, ultimately, to take me back home, where he believed I would be his to control again.

"You've said that before." Two's laugh was rough and forced. "Why should I believe you this time?"

We traded back and forth, me trying to defuse instead of ignite this time and Two trying to decide which way to move.

In the end I said, "Leave Jack alone and we'll go home together," and believed it. Anything to keep Jack safe.

"You sound honest. All right. We'll go home together. But to stop you from running off again . . ." Two's arm thrust forwards.

Jack arched, sucking in a sudden breath. My heart stopped, then burst into furious life when he screamed a second later.

The rifle was at the ready without thought. "Jack!"

Two laughed and pulled his knife free of Jack's body, bloody drops spraying through the pale moonlight. He shoved Jack so he toppled down the cement stairs to the cages.

My blood had boiled when Two killed Nine. Now, it turned to ice.

"You're going to die, Two. I promise you."

His laugh was joyous. Dismissive. Taunting.

I opened fire but he was already moving. Pistol in each hand, he returned the shots. His vision issues were mitigated by our proximity and the fact he was wearing NV gear. We circled the pit, exchanging shots. I wanted to get to Jack, to make sure he was still alive, but Two knew that and worked to keep me away. At least until he could be certain there would be nothing I could do to help Jack. It had always been his MO. Hurt me, then offer comfort. It made me sick to think of how often I'd fallen for it.

Of course, his other goal was to waste our ammunition, so if I wanted to continue this, I would have to close with him, where he had all the advantage.

Exactly what Nine and Seven had warned me against.

When the bullets were starting to run low, Two interspersed his shots with verbal ammunition, trying to make me reminisce about the good times with him. His mistake was believing I remembered those times fondly.

Finally Two reverted to his earlier tactic. "Come on, baby brother. Let's agree to disagree and just go home. I promise I'll—"

I fired and Two grunted and staggered. I moved rapidly, getting closer.

"You little shit," Two snarled.

Another shot but he ducked this time. His movements proved I'd landed a hit, but it also sent him into what cover he could find. A pity because I was rapidly running out of bullets.

"Give up," I advised coolly. "You're wounded. I'm not. Time to end this."

Two laughed. "You think a couple of grazes are going to slow me down? You've never beaten me. Never." He used his words to cover his shift into the ruins beyond the pit.

There was too much open space to cross without exposing myself to whatever ammunition he had left. One last chance to flush him out. I fired my final rounds moving between each one, and yet Two still managed to locate me when I came to a stop again. Still too far back to risk rushing him.

"Last shots. I've been counting."

"And you even kept your shoes on."

Two snarled. "Just like you, but at least I'm not ashamed of my feet."

I had no chance to respond to the taunt because it spurred Jack into action instead.

Movement from the pit and a dull silver shape arced out and flew towards Two's position. "Ma petite erreur," Jack shouted at the same time.

Meaning hit me almost instantaneously.

Eyes squeezed shut, intense white light flared beyond my lids even as I was moving. Two screamed, scrabbling over the broken blocks of the ruins, guiding me.

I had learned quickly when I'd first joined the group of Sugar Babies how to map a space fast while blind. How to move around and over obstacles rapidly, often fleeing for my life from one sibling or another. It was a skill I'd not let atrophy, even after I'd been given my sight. Perpetual darkness had never been something Two had had to learn to live with.

So he faltered. He stumbled and his long limbs worked against him. I followed the noises he made and closed with him.

It didn't take long because for once, I had the biggest advantage.

I was finally fighting to kill my brother.

They didn't let me go with Jack to the hospital. He went one way in an ambulance, sirens screaming and lights flashing, and I went the other, cuffed and locked into the back of an Office SUV. Two's and Jack's blood was still wet on my hands.

No one gave me any updates on Jack's condition all the way back to Darling Harbour. Not even when they took me below ground and ushered me into a cell.

I didn't ask. Didn't resist. Didn't allow myself any room to feel anything. I was back in the enemy's stronghold with no exit strategy and no Jack. Towards dawn, I realised I didn't even particularly care if I never left the cell again. So long as Two never got to hurt another person. So long as Jack was all right. Especially if Jack didn't make it.

Director Tan opened the door to the cell midmorning. "Mr. Blade," he said urbanely. "So sorry for the delay, but there were discussions to be had. I'm sure you understand."

I stared at him, unmoving.

"Mr. Reardon is okay. He came through the surgery very well and has just arrived into our infirmary. Something about anaesthetic making him very talkative, I believe." When that failed to move me, he added, "I've come to take you to see him."

They didn't cuff me. Tan even waved off the security detail that tried to fall in around us, murmuring assurances as he guided me along the corridor I had once fought my way down.

The infirmary was on another subterranean level. Ten beds lined two walls of a sterile room. Jack lay in the one closest to the door, Quinn in the one next in line. Between them sat Lewis, head bowed as he flicked a finger over the screen of his phone. Director Tan waited outside, letting me enter alone, although there was a large observation window in the wall and he and the medical staff all watched regardless.

"Hey," Lewis said softly when he saw me. "He's okay. Just sleeping off the sedatives."

I stopped at the end of Jack's bed. He looked peaceful, like he was simply sleeping in on a lazy morning. Black curls tangled together on the white pillow, his brown skin had lost some of its usual depth of colour, but his chest rose and fell smoothly. The need to crawl into the bed beside him was incredibly strong.

Lewis put his phone away and stood as well, looking down at his best friend, then up at me. "How are you doing?"

He sounded genuinely concerned. I had no idea how much Jack had told him about us—about me—but he was an Office asset and had to know enough to have an opinion about Ethan Blade regardless. And that opinion seemed to be favourable. A single lock deep inside clicked open.

I could only nod at him. He smiled, then moved past me and went to organise water and a towel, so I could clean up. When the dried blood was washed away, I touched Jack. He was very warm, but that was because I felt so cold.

Awareness prickled against my nerves. Looking up, I found Quinn awake and staring at me with hollow eyes in a pale face. I didn't know him, but I had watched him. Studied him. Stalked him. The man in the bed was not the man who'd pursued Jack over the past weeks. I felt sorry that Quinn had been hurt by Two, but I couldn't feel sorry *for* him. Didn't know if I ever would.

All too soon, I was asked to leave the infirmary so the staff could tend their patients. Lewis came with me and sat in on the meetings with the directors and the director in charge. He spoke up on my behalf several times, argued points with the directors, and kept sending me hopeful smiles when the negotiations went my way.

"Why are you helping me?" I asked when it was over and I was allowed to walk alone out of the meeting room.

Lewis gave a small shrug. "I'm not sure about you yet. I mean, you've been one of our top priority subjects for years. But Jack trusts you. He doesn't do that easily, so it means a lot to me." He stopped and made sure we were alone. "But, as his best friend, I have to tell you that if you hurt him? I'm coming for you with every resource the Office can muster. Okay?"

I smiled.

"Good." Lewis fist bumped my shoulder. "Let's go see if he's awake yet."

Quinn was gone went we got to the infirmary. He'd been released, undoubtedly only after signing a wad of non-disclosure agreements that made similar promises as Lewis's to me if he dared speak about anything he'd experienced or seen.

Jack was sleeping. The nurse in attendance said he'd been in and out all day and assured us he would be fine. Lewis sat with me for a while, then when his yawns got so big I could see his back molars, he shuffled off, advising me to get some sleep as well.

I had been awake for over forty-eight hours by that point and tiredness was dragging at my arms and legs. I felt weary and vulnerable. I was within the clutches of the enemy.

I gave in and crawled into bed with Jack. There was a moment of resistance, but then I laid my head on his shoulder and he shifted towards me in his sleep.

And I fell asleep.

CODA

Dejana gripped the armrests of her seat as the plane wobbled in a small patch of turbulence, the silent pilot steadying the craft skilfully once they were through, allowing her to relax again. After two hectic car chases that day, she didn't need any more excitement.

Even though she worked in incredibly dangerous circles, that was the closest she had ever come to being caught. All for one megabyte of data about a secret Australian SAS mission in India no one had ever cared about before. Which could only mean one thing. Someone—maybe the Cabal, maybe not—had decided they didn't want anyone else knowing about how half a dozen soldiers had died on foreign soil.

But she was free now. On her way to the next safe port, where she would change identity once again and disappear. She was so relieved to have escaped she would actually do as she promised and cut Saint free of the Cabal.

The plane juddered again and Dejana tensed. "Andre, is there going to be much more turbulence?"

He didn't answer, not even when they steadied up again.

"Andre?"

The pilot shifted in his seat but she couldn't see anything more than the back of his dark-haired head and a gloved hand on the stick between black clad legs.

"I get it," Dejana said soothingly. "I know I didn't give you much notice. I promise to make it up to you. Three times your usual amount." When all she got was more silence, she added, "Four times. Surely that's enough to cover the inconvenience."

"I'm sure it is."

Dejana gasped. That wasn't Andre's New Zealand accent. "Who are you? Where's Andre?"

"At home with his family," the monotonal British voice answered. The pilot turned in his seat and pointed a giant handgun right at her. He appeared to be Middle Eastern, or South Asian, but his eyes were the white of a Sugar Baby. "The Cabal wants you to know they appreciate all the work you've done for them over the years, but you've betrayed them one too many times."

Well, she had been close.

Bang!

Ten days after I killed Two, Jack put on his service dress uniform and after I'd pinned his medals to his chest, left for Senior Sergeant Stephanie Phelps's funeral. He invited me to go with him, but I wouldn't feel comfortable amongst so many law enforcement officers, nor the sergeant's family. If I had been smarter, worked it out sooner, she wouldn't be dead. Quite apart from my guilt, I had my own task as well.

My first voluntary visit to the Office without Jack, or nefarious reason, went well. Director Tan met with me in the underground garage and escorted me to the first subbasement, where my packages were waiting. He offered, once again, to have the remains of my sister interred in a military cemetery. An unnamed soldier, he assured me, so she received respect instead of condemnation. There was no such offer for Two, so I turned him down again.

Taking both their ashes, I went to the cemetery and picked up Jack. He was sad and troubled, partly because Dr. Adam Quinn was leaving with a tortured expression on his face. We followed him to the airport to give Jack some small measure of closure, then we returned to Middle Head.

I had picked this place not because it was where I'd killed Two, but because it was special. To history, to Sydney—to Jack.

It was sunset when we reached the end of the point. Jack's hand was a comforting pressure on the base of my spine. His own sorrow had been put aside and he was here for me.

Nine and Two weren't the first of my siblings I'd lost. There had been thirteen in the group after I joined them. Eleven of us had survived to the final test. Six of us had made it through in order to be released into the world to do the Cabal's bidding. I'd never been to a funeral for any of them, though.

I had also never felt this dull weight in my belly like a rock trying to pull me under an ever-shifting surface. Over the past week it had felt as if one moment I could breathe and in another, I couldn't. Guilt or grief, I wasn't certain, but it had torn at my control. As always, Jack had been a comfort, but that old worry that I would come to rely too heavily on him had reared its head. So I'd driven instead. Long, long drives into the country, chasing a peace I'd never been able to catch.

Maybe here, at the end of the land, I'd finally find it.

Jack, seemingly reading my heart better than I did, let me walk the last few meters on my own. He held onto Two's urn, leaving me to say my farewell to Nine alone. My sibling in every way except for blood. Given the order, she would have tried to kill me, but until that point, she had been my sister. My companion in this strange life we'd been given. My friend.

Nine had died because of me.

Me. One-three. The only one in our group who'd sworn to never kill one of the others, no matter who gave the order. I may not have broken her neck, but it was me who'd brought her here. Me who'd asked her to go against Two knowing he had the better chance. Me who'd put my own happiness ahead of her life.

Don't be an idiot. She chose to do it.

The thought sounded so much like her it made me smile. It was true. If she hadn't wanted to help me, she most certainly wouldn't have. Not even for all the peppermint crisp tart in the world.

"I'm going to miss you, sister," I whispered. "I'm so sorry for everything that's happened. I'm sorry that you came here for me, and he killed you. I'm so incredibly sorry for what *they* did to you. To all of us."

Before me, the water was darkening as the last reflected rays of the sun faded away. While there was still a touch of golden colour in the sky, I opened the urn and, as a breeze eddied around me, tipped it up.

"You spent your life in the dark, sister. Now you can be in the light."

Nine's ashes tumbled out and the wind caught them, carrying them out into the last of the daylight. The weight didn't lessen as the ashes dissipated. I wasn't sure it ever would ease. Wasn't sure if it ever should.

Easy goodbye done, I held out a hand to Jack and he came to me, urn ready to exchange. Instead, I wound my arm around his neck. It was instinct. I hurt so I sought safe shelter. Jack's arm was hard and secure around me, his breath warm on the cold skin of my cheek.

"Whatever you need," he murmured, voice thick with emotion.

The promise in his words rocked through me and I held on tighter. The weight shifted inside, not so it was any lighter, but it felt . . . easier to carry. Easier to do this.

I swapped the empty urn for the full one and Jack went to step away.

"Stay with me." Just because I didn't want to be dependent on him didn't mean I didn't need him. Especially now.

"Of course." Jack moved behind me, one arm across my chest.

There were no words this time. Nothing could encompass how I felt about Two and what I felt as the one who'd killed him. I didn't even know what I felt. Or if I should feel it at all. The only thing I knew for certain was that I needed this finished. So I opened Two's urn and set him free. It hurt, like the knife I'd stabbed into him.

"I shouldn't . . ." Hurt. Miss him. Mourn him. "Not after everything he did."

"It's okay. You don't need to excuse your feelings."

No. But it didn't answer why I had to feel them at all.

I dropped the urn over the cliff, wanting the last of my brother to be gone. And because carrying it back to the car felt too much, I sent Nine's urn after it.

Both arms free, Jack held me tighter. Everything inside me was blank, or such a whirling mess all the different shades blended into black. Only when the rest of the light had bled out of the world and it matched the darkness inside could I think again.

"What do we do now, Jack?"

"Anything you want."

The heat in his voice was like a bonfire in the dark. It licked through me like flames, banishing the cold night. The weight in my belly took on a different feel. Warmer. More insistent. Magnetic, pulling towards the man behind me. I let it guide me, let it draw my arms around his neck and press me as close to his body as I could get.

"Anything?" My voice dropped into a husky rumble.

Jack battled against a smile, but lost when I tipped his uniform hat off the back of his head. The smile was sweet but debauched, patient but expectant. Supportive but nervous. He could charm me so easily. No wonder I loved this contrary, stubborn, beautiful man.

"Hmm, but there is so much I want . . ." A home. A life I chose for myself. Freedom. But most of all—him.

And he gave me everything the moment his lips touched mine.

ACKNOWLEDGEMENTS

As always, many, many thanks to Erin McLellan, Layla Reyne and Anna Zabo for all the support and help, and May Peterson for bringing her talent to my words once again and the very patient L.C. Chase for another wonderful cover.

ALSO BY L.J. HAYWARD

M/M Romantic Suspense

Death and the Devil Series
Where Death Meets the Devil, #1
Where Death Meets the Devil: Coda, #1.2
Bargaining with the Devil, #1.4
When the Devil Drives, #1.6
Devil in the Details, #1.8
Why the Devil Stalks Death, #2

Urban Fantasy

Night Call Series
Blood Work, #1
Demon Dei, #2
Here Be Dragons, #2.5
Rock Paper Sorcery, #3

ABOUT THE AUTHOR

L.J. Hayward has been telling stories for most of her life, a good deal of them of the tall variety. She loves reading but doesn't seem to have enough time between wanting to be a more disciplined writer, being the actual erratic writer she is, and working for dollars in a dungeon laboratory. She also lives on the Gold Coast in Queensland, but rarely sees a beach and can't surf, though she thinks living on a houseboat might be fun. At least then she'd have an excuse to get a cat.

Visit L.J. at her website, ljhayward.com; on Twitter, @ljhayward; or on Goodreads, goodreads.com/L.J.Hayward.